CW00866426

THE HOUSE ABOVE THE RIVER

Giles Armitage needed to get away from it all and a sailing holiday with friends was just the escape he needed. Everything was going well until they became stranded in thick fog. Luckily they were invited to stay at a small château nearby, until the weather cleared.

But the atmosphere in the château was tense. Giles was brought face to face with the woman he once loved, and whom he was trying to forget—the hauntingly beautiful Miriam. Miriam's husband was clearly uneasy and she was terrified—convinced, as she confided in Giles, that someone was trying to kill her. Following a series of disturbing accidents, Giles began to think she could possibly be right.

THE HOUSE ABOVE THE RIVER

Josephine Bell

·BLACK·
DAGGER
·CRIME·

First published in Great Britain 1959
by
Hodder & Stoughton Ltd
This edition 1991 by Chivers Press
published by arrangement with
the author's estate

ISBN 0 86220 802 5

British Library Cataloguing in Publication Data

Bell, Josephine, *1897–1987*
 The house above the river.
 I. Title
 823.912

ISBN 0–86220–802–5

Note

The château, the village of Penguerrec, and all of the characters in
this book are fictitious. The rest of the geography of Brittany described, including the Tréguier river (apart from Penguerrec) is
factual.

Printed and bound in Great Britain by
Redwood Press Limited, Melksham, Wiltshire

FOREWORD

I WAS ONCE locked into a prison cell with Josephine Bell. The incident took place in York Police Headquarters in 1979 and was not, I hasten to add, because we were both apprehended felons. We had been attending a Crime Writers' Association conference in York and were kindly being shown around by the then Chief Constable of North Yorkshire, Mr Kenneth Henshaw.

Whilst we languished companionably behind bars, Miss Bell revealed her feelings about British crime-writing, expressing the opinion that she did not want to see it slip into a pattern of mere violence and sex as American crime novels were tending to do. 'In my early days,' she told me, 'there was no sex in crime novels. In sensitive places we put a series of dots—now we have to know how to spell the naughty words. As far as I am concerned a crime novel should pose the questions "who dunnit" and "why did they do it" not "who did they do it with".'

It was a rule of thumb from which, luckily for her readers, she never deviated.

When *The House Above the River* was first published in 1959, Josephine Bell had been writing for 23 years. She was a Grande Dame of the genre, her name ranking alongside Margery Allingham, Ngaio Marsh, Dorothy L. Sayers and other greats of the Golden Age of Detective Fiction. A founder member of the Crime Writers' Association, in 1959 she was the Association's much respected chairman.

The House Above the River is not of the Great Detective school of crime fiction. It is not dominated by a super-sleuth in the mould of Poirot or Maigret. It is crime fiction of the classic puzzle variety, heavily laced with romantic suspense and spiced with a chilling touch of the Gothic.

In the late 1950s Romantic Suspense was riding high. Mary Stewart's first novel *Madam, Will You Talk* had been published in 1955 and had struck a deep chord with a large readership. Josephine Bell possessed every trait that made the Stewart novels so popular. She evokes a sense of place, in this case the colourful fishing ports of Brittany, with consummate skill and, without detracting in the slightest from the main thrust of the storyline, she portrays the kind of hero we would all like to have on our side in a time of crisis, and she sustains the mystery until the last page.

In *The House Above the River*, Josephine Bell indulges her love of all things nautical and puts her knowledge of all things medical (she was a doctor like many of her family), to good use. The hero is Giles Armitage. Holidaying with two friends, Tony and Phillipa Marshall, he is sailing his yacht, the *Shuna*, along the Brittany coastline. As heavy fog descends he navigates with difficulty into the mouth of the Tréguier river, anchoring below the house of the title, an unkempt and neglected, though inhabited, château.

Unpleasant shocks are in store for Giles. He and his companions are invited to the château by Susan Brockley, a pretty young English girl. Susan is a cousin of the owner, Henry Davenport, and when she introduces Giles to the sickly Henry and to Henry's dramatically beautiful wife Miriam, Giles is stunned to find himself confronting the woman to whom he was once engaged; the woman who nearly destroyed him when she walked out on him.

His one desire is now to walk out on her, but Miriam Davenport is a woman obsessed by fear, a woman who sees him as her only Saviour. Slowly and inescapably Giles and his companions are sucked into a vortex of evil, enmeshed in a web of malice and greed and revenge and hatred. Murder is the inevitable conclusion. But murder of whom? By whom? And for why?

Without depicting excessive violence or the distasteful and distracting sex scenes of which she was so disdainful, Josephine Bell keeps the reader hooked and teased until the last page. There can be no better recipe for a good book.

MARGARET PEMBERTON

Margaret Pemberton has served twice on the CWA Committee and she has also been Chairman of the Romantic Novelists' Association. Her two dozen novels cover romantic suspense, family sagas and historical and contemporary tales, set in all parts of the world, and often reaching the bestseller lists. She travels widely and her interests range from Elizabethan drama to ocean sailing.

THE BLACK DAGGER CRIME SERIES

The Black Dagger Crime series is a result of a joint effort between Chivers Press and a sub-committee of the Crime Writers' Association, consisting of Marian Babson, Peter Chambers and chaired by John Kennedy Melling. It is designed to select outstanding examples of every type of detective story, so that enthusiasts will have the opportunity to read once more classics that have been scarce for years, while at the same time introducing them to a new generation who have not previously had the chance to enjoy them.

CHAPTER I

THE FOG ROLLED in from the sea behind them, blotting out the leading marks and blurring the rocks close at hand. The wind, that had lessened for the last three hours, died as the mist came, leaving the yacht's sails limp, drooping in a clammy silence.

Giles Armitage swore, Tony Marshall went below to start up the auxiliary engine. Phillipa, Tony's wife, exclaimed in exasperation, "It *would* catch us up just here, of all places."

Giles only said, "What do we have next? You take over the book of words, Pip."

The Stuart Turner engine broke the silence with a satisfactorily steady mutter, and Tony clambered back into the cockpit.

"Go up for'ard and look out for snags," Giles told him. "We have to turn off almost at right angles about here. Tell him the marks, Pip."

Busily reading from Hasler's invaluable guide to the Brittany coast, Phillipa gave the names and positions of the various buoys and beacons that marked the complicated entrance through the rocks to the Tréguier river. Giles, who knew his compass course from the chart, tried desperately to remember how far the set of the tide would carry him off it, now that the sea fog had hidden the distant transit. Without visible leading marks it would be a tricky business groping their way round La Corne lighthouse to the line of buoys that marked the entrance of the river itself. If only the wind had held an hour longer, or had died a couple of hours before they made the rocks and lighthouse of Les Heaux. They could have hung about then, safely out at sea, until the fog cleared. But it had been a wonderful passage in record time from the Needles which they had left at dawn the morning before, with a steady northerly wind behind them. The splendid lighthouses of the north Brittany coast had shone out of a clear night. Only when

they began to close the coast with the newly-risen sun glittering across the water, the wind had begun to slacken. Perhaps
he should have used the motor then to keep up his speed. But
there seemed to be no point in it, with another lovely summer
day before them, and the whole of a fortnight's holiday ahead.
No point at all, until that low soft yellow line wiped out the
horizon, and caught them up at the landward end of the first
part of the Grand Channel leading to Tréguier.

The yacht *Shuna* crept forward. Tony, leaning out from the
pulpit in the bows, saw a dim black shape ahead. He shouted
his warning, but Giles had seen the buoy almost as soon as his
crew, and had altered course to pass it.

"Fine," he shouted, cheerfully. He was pleased to pass the
mark so close, even if the tide was pushing him on to it. This
was where he had to alter course, and he could check his
position quite accurately on the chart. Also he could see
exactly how the set ran on the buoy and make a reasonable
guess of how to correct for it in the next reach of the channel.

"How often have you been in here?" asked Phillipa.

Her voice had a sharp note of anxiety in it that Giles was
quick to note.

"Hundreds of times," he said, heartily.

This was not true. He had, in fact, used this channel only
twice before. But he remembered it fairly well, and he saw
that he must keep up the morale of his crew. The Marshalls
had not done much cruising. They had been too excited all the
long day before to take proper rests. Tony had stood up to his
night watch without turning a hair, and had slept well when
relieved. But Phillipa, though fortified with dramamine, had
not slept at all when she went below, and had soon appeared
again on deck, queasy, but uncomplaining, to sit up for the
rest of the night. She was looking pinched and tired now, Giles
thought, and must on no account be frightened into the
bargain.

"It's lifting!" Tony shouted suddenly from the bows. "I
can see a couple of socking great beacons. Look!"

The fog swirled and broke and they shot out into a clear
patch a few hundred yards long. They could not see the shore

line to the left, but on the right a formidable pile of rocks, not far away, rose from the water. The beacons stood on the edge of this barrier.

Giles altered course again. He had not allowed enough for the set, but he did so now, and was rewarded, twenty minutes later, by spotting his next mark where it ought to be. The fog was a little denser again here, but they still had a couple of hundred yards visibility. At any rate, Giles thought, we are not likely to run into any other shipping larger than ourselves. The little summer passenger steamer would not leave the river until the fog lifted. Once past La Corne . . .

The in-shore lighthouse, on its spit of rock, came out of the mist, a pale tall ghost, dead ahead, and very uncomfortably close, since they knew they must give it a fairly wide berth, and the current was now setting them down on it very fast. Giles opened the throttle, and *Shuna* roared away to starboard, slipping past the rocky base of La Corne almost broadside on to the channel.

"I can see two buoys ahead here," called Tony.

"Thank God for that!"

Giles slowed down again, glancing at Phillipa as he did so. Her face was very white, and he cursed himself for the exaggerated note of relief he had not been able to keep out of his voice.

"You go up in the bows with Tony," he said, quietly. "Help him count the buoys till we turn off to port. It's only sand now, but I don't want to stick on it. After this reach we turn off, and then the tide will take us straight into the river. Nearly there, now."

She gave him a wan smile and went forward to her husband's side. Giles checked his new course, praying that the fog would not thicken until they were safely in the river. These coastal fog patches could do anything. They came suddenly and unexpectedly as this one had, and they lifted just as unpredictably. Perhaps it was a clear, sunny morning in Tréguier. Perhaps there was no visibility there at all. They would soon know.

The fog might have been arranged to tantalise them. As they reached the river mouth it lifted almost completely, and they had a sudden lovely vision of Pen Paluch on their right, the houses climbing up the hill, the fishing boats lying at anchor, the green-gold fields beyond. On the other side, in the sun's eye, was the woody slope of the hill above the river, and the smaller village of Penguerrec clustered about the mouth of a little creek, with more fishing boats riding the gentle swell. But as they drove forward into the narrowing waters, trees, hills, villages, boats, and even the river itself, were swallowed up in a mist far denser than anything they had so far met. It wrapped them up completely, cold and wet as rain. They could not even see the full length of the yacht.

"Hell and damnation!" cried Giles, exasperated beyond measure.

His crew scrambled aft into the cockpit. Giles grinned at them ruefully.

"We're here," he said. "We've only got to drop the hook where we won't dry out at low tide. *Only!*"

Tony went back to the foredeck to prepare the anchor and anchor chain; Phillipa stood by with the lead line, ready to take the depth of the water when Giles gave the word. From the way he had spoken she felt sure he knew every inch of this river. And anyway they were in. The great fanged rocks had not seized them on their groping passage. She felt great relief, and she was so tired she could hardly move.

"Something ahead," called Tony, in an uncertain voice, breaking the silence.

"What sort of something, you clot?"

"Flat. I can't see. . . . Yes, I can. A landing-stage."

"*Landing-stage?*" Giles put the engine into neutral, and while *Shuna* slid gently forward, searched the chart and Hasler's book. "I don't see any . . ."

"Bear away!" called Tony, "unless you want to ram it."

The yacht swung away, and a minute later they slid past a neat well-kept little landing-stage of wooden planks, to which a smart, varnished dinghy and a small, white-painted motor launch were tied.

"Good enough," Giles said, cheerfully. "Do your stuff, Pip. I'll go on a bit and turn and we'll stop as near that thing as we can make. This fog can't last for ever, and the day is still very young. We'll go on up to the town when it's cleared."

He found a position where they were in the deep channel of the river, clear of the mud, and dropped anchor. The two men fixed the anchor chain, Phillipa gathered up the charts, torches, navigation aids, empty mugs and other remains of their passage, and took them below. She could hardly keep her eyes open, but she knew her duty was urgent, and set to at once to make breakfast. Tension had been too high on their approach through the rocks for any of them to think of it until now. She cooked a generous meal of bacon and eggs, and insisted upon the men going below to eat it hot, though they protested they had not finished tidying up on deck. •

"It can wait," she insisted, and for once Giles took this heresy meekly.

After breakfast, still wrapped in the stillness of the fog, but secure in the knowledge that they lay off the course of anything larger than a small fishing boat, they all turned in, and slept the undreaming sleep of effort rewarded.

Phillipa woke first. She and Tony shared the cabin, while Giles occupied a quarter-berth further aft, opposite the galley. Gathering her clothes together, she went forward into the fore-peak, moving noiselessly to avoid waking the two men. She dressed quickly, and climbed on deck through the fore-hatch, drawing in a quick breath of pleasure at what she saw.

It was now four o'clock in the afternoon, her watch told her. The fog had gone, and a brilliant sun was turning the sandy mud of the river bank to gold. The leaves of the trees beyond glinted and sparkled as they moved in a light breeze blowing in from the sea. Further off, on the same side of the river as *Shuna*, were the moored fishing boats they had seen for that brief instant as they came in. She could see now that they lay off a sloping hard, where rowing boats were drawn up, and beyond which steps and a sea wall led to a winding road, bordered by stone cottages.

It was the sort of scene she had looked forward to, never before having sailed on the Brittany coast. It was what Tony and Giles had raved about all the winter, planning this cruise.

Here it was, then, at last, reminding her of Cornwall or Devon, but with a character of its own, an exciting strangeness, that made her want to go ashore at once, to explore the village and meet the people, some of whom she could see, small in the distance, and slow moving, on the grey rock of the hard below the sea wall.

She turned to look in the other direction, up the river, and there was the landing-stage, fifty yards away, with the varnished dinghy and the gleaming white launch, the trees dropping to the bend of the river. The whole thing might have been a stretch of the Thames near Goring, she thought.

"Want to go ashore?"

Phillipa turned quickly and laughed.

"That stage looks terribly private," she said. "I miss the 'No landing' notice."

Giles laughed.

"I don't see why we shouldn't use it, as it *doesn't* have a notice. It's a hell of a way back to Penguerrec."

"Is that the village on this side?"

"Yes. Pen Paluch further seaward on the other bank. You can't really see it at the moment; it's straight into the sun."

Phillipa screwed up her eyes and then looked away, dazzled.

"If we go ashore we could get some milk and bread. I've no fresh milk left, and I'm down to rock bottom in bread."

"Right. You go and rouse out Tony. Tell him I want a hand getting the dinghy down into the water."

Presently Phillipa and her husband went off to the landing-stage, the former taking a milk can and a large haversack for provisions. Giles watched them tie up and disappear among the trees, waving goodbye to him as they took what he decided must be a definite path up the hill.

When they had gone he turned to various small jobs on deck. These had been his excuse for staying on board, but they were not inventions. The sails, still wet from the fog, needed drying out. He spread the mainsail in the sun, and hoisted the jib to flap in the gentle breeze. He tidied up ends of rope, oiled the winches, tinkered for half an hour with the Stuart Turner, though it had given no trouble on this occasion, and finally, lighting a pipe, sat down in the cockpit to enjoy the sun and the scenery, and a sense of mild achievement.

A small grey fishing boat passed him, coming down river from Tréguier, making for the hard at Penguerrec. There were a man and a boy in it, who stared at him as they passed, but did not speak to him until he called to ask them if he was in a good position where he had anchored. The man nodded, and grinned widely. As he chugged on, Giles heard him say something in the Breton dialect to the boy, who shouted with laughter.

The tide that had carried them into the river early that morning, had turned at eleven, and was now near the bottom of the ebb. The fall was about thirty feet, so that the banks now seemed very high. The landing-stage, Giles saw, was built in three sections, one fixed, and two floating. As the latter sank with the water, iron ladders appeared, leading vertically from one to the next. The floating sections moved up and down on iron rings round posts, pontoon fashion. The ladders must be slimy and slippery when the water sank away from them, he thought, though by now they had dried in the sun. He understood why the boats fastened to the stage had been tied to the section furthest out in the river. This part was still floating, though the launch appeared to be aground.

Giles went below to sort out his charts and put them away. Presently he heard a shout, and going on deck saw Tony and Phillipa waving to him from the stage.

There was a girl with them. He saw that she was slim and tall, nearly as tall as Tony, and that she had fair hair, glinting in the sun like the leaves of the trees behind her. He was too far off to see her face clearly.

He stood up in the cockpit and waved back, hoping his crew had not asked the stranger aboard. He had come to Brittany to enjoy sailing and scenery and to get away from the exactions of his work. Not to begin a social round. He had no objection to visiting old friends on other yachts; he was sure to meet some of them in the course of the trip. But strange girls, provincial French at that, and on the very first day . . . !

Tony and Phillipa had some difficulty getting down the second ladder with the shopping. It seemed to be still very slippery. They had more difficulty getting the dinghy away from the stage. Their weight sank it in the mud, for the water was very shallow where they had tied up. The fair-haired girl climbed lightly down the ladder to shove them off, and then stood for a minute or two watching as they moved away. Phillipa called goodbye, and the girl answered in an unmistakably English voice, and turning quickly, went back up both ladders and disappeared among the trees.

"Who was that?" Giles asked, when his crew were on board again.

"We met her in the village," said Phillipa. "She's English."

"So I heard," said Giles.

"Her cousin owns the house—it's a small château, really, in the woods there. And the landing-stage is his. We ran into her first on the road to the village."

"It was rather funny," Tony explained. "We asked her in our very limited French if she knew where we could get milk and things, and she told us, also in French. Then a bit later, when we'd got everything in the village and were coming back, and had just turned off into the wood, we met her again."

"She told us we were trespassing, and we tried to explain, but our French didn't run to it, and then she laughed and said she was English, too."

"She allowed you to go on trespassing, I gather?" Giles suggested.

"Yes, indeed. She seemed quite pleased we'd come. She took us back up the road to the main gate of the house, and showed us a path from it that joins the one we took from the landing-stage, which incidentally peters out half-way up the hill. She came right down with us."

"So I saw," said Giles, sourly. A provincial French girl would have been bad enough, but a fellow-countrywoman was the end.

"You couldn't have seen very clearly," said Phillipa, "or you wouldn't say it like that. She's terribly pretty, isn't she, Tony? Really, quite beautiful."

"She most certainly is. I'd have asked her to come off for tea on board, only she wouldn't have been able to get back comfortably for several hours. I thought we were going to have to wait, ourselves. We three on board the dinghy would have stuck."

"Tides have many uses," said Giles.

Tony and Phillipa exchanged glances, but said nothing. The latter began to sort out the food she had bought.

Later in the evening, Giles said, "I suppose you thanked that girl for letting you use her stage?"

"Her cousin's stage," said Tony.

"Same thing."

"Not really. She doesn't live here. Only staying the summer."

"Really? Had she any right, then, to give you permission to go through the grounds?"

Phillipa interrupted.

"The cousin and his wife are away in Paris. I imagine she's in charge. Until tonight, that is. She said they'd be back."

She did not add that Susan Brockley had invited them all to the château for coffee in the morning. That could wait until the skipper was in a better mood.

"I see." Giles's manner expressed total indifference. "Not that it matters," he said. "We'll run up to Tréguier in the morning and have a look round and lunch at a place I know where they give you a damned good meal. Then on to Lézardrieux in the afternoon."

But the next morning they woke to find *Shuna* wrapped round by a fog much denser than the one through which they had entered the river the day before. It lifted a little towards noon, and they could see the landing-stage dimly in the mist. But by then it was too late to carry out any of the plan Giles had put before them so confidently the night before.

CHAPTER II

"I'LL HAVE TO do some more shopping," said Phillipa. "We may be stuck here for days. Susan told us the fog banks often lie over the sea for a week at a time, when it's brilliant weather on land."

Giles, who knew this only too well, merely said, "We'll row down to the hard."

"But we can't see it."

"We can find it."

"What's the objection to the landing-stage?" Tony asked. "We've got permission."

"Not from the owner."

"If his cousin has given us leave I don't suppose he'll be surly about it. Why should he? Fellow-countrymen and all."

The argument continued for a few minutes, but was settled when Phillipa said, "If we don't go soon we shall never get back in time for lunch. Anyway, the tide will be much too strong to row against coming back from the hard. So let's get going, and use the stage."

She stepped down into the dinghy with the shopping bags and milk can, and the men followed. Tony took the oars and set off for the landing-stage. Giles only said, "The tide is flooding till twelve noon," and left it at that.

They met no one on the walk up through the wood. As they mounted, the mist cleared, and the sun began to stream through the branches. When they came to a fork in the path, Phillipa pointed to the left.

"That goes up to the house," she said. "It gets wider a bit further on, with rhododendrons and azalea bushes, and marvellous hydrangeas in flower. Very wild, though. We didn't see anything like a real garden, did we, Tony?"

"If you mean a lawn, no. But quite a lot of roses."

"What about this path?" Giles asked, pointing to the right.

"That comes out on the road. It's the one we went up

14

yesterday. It sort of peters out further up, and the brambles are wicked."

Giles strode ahead on the right hand path. The delay in the cruise was infuriating, but there was nothing to be done about it. If the fog lifted he could take *Shuna* up the river on the engine later in the afternoon. In the meantime there was this village to explore. A meagre substitute for the day he had planned. But he accepted frustration. He had come to believe it was inevitable.

The path brought them into a rough field bordered by a bramble hedge. Beyond this a gate led into a narrow road. They climbed the gate and turned left towards the village.

"You see," said Phillipa, pulling off her cardigan. "Bright clear sky, no wind, no mist. Glorious summer."

"Hellishly hot," grumbled Tony.

"Take off that thick sweater, then."

"I haven't got a shirt on."

"Penguerrec won't mind a naked torso. Just another mad Englishman. Anyway, Giles is respectable enough for two."

Dear Giles, she thought, glancing sideways at him. He always manages to look marvellous in any circumstances. He was wearing fawn slacks and a thin russet-coloured shirt, that went admirably with his brown face and nearly black hair. No wonder the village girls turned to stare after him as they passed. Such a pity he never even wanted to speak to a woman if he could help it. Such a pity: such a waste.

The road dipped to the river, going round in a wide curve. They dropped back into the mist, through which the low roofs of the village appeared dimly.

"I want to get round to the hard," said Phillipa, "and see if I can find some lobsters and what they call seafruit."

"Judging by what you get in Tréguier," said Giles, "you ought to find plenty of oysters and such. You go ahead. I must send off some postcards, if I can find any. Did you come across a post office yesterday?"

"Further on," said Phillipa. "All the shops are in one wide street. The church is at the end of it. The post office is just beyond the shops. A grey front, with a few notices on it."

"Right," said Giles. "Are you going with Pip, Tony?"

"I'll go to carry back the homards," he answered.

"More likely to be langoustines," Giles told him. "Or spider crabs. You'll probably be given them alive, too."

"Then I think I'll stick to oysters," said Phillipa, shuddering.

She and Tony turned off along a road that seemed to lead on towards the sea, and Giles went up, climbing again into the sunshine.

He was writing the addresses on his postcards in the post office, when he heard a clear voice, in an unmistakably English accent, asking for stamps. He looked up. The girl with the shining hair, and it still shone, he noted, even in the subdued light of the post office, stood beside him, struggling with the currency.

Phillipa had said she was pretty, even beautiful, he remembered. She was not, by his standard. But then his standard had been fixed so long ago. Fixed for good; for bad, really. He ought to change it, by force of will, if possible. Phillipa said the girl was beautiful. Her hair was yellow, she probably had blue eyes to go with it, the cheek he could see was a clear gold-brown, the make-up pleasing. All right, then, she was pretty.

With a violent recoil from such a conclusion, he turned back to his postcards, but when he looked up again, she was still there, facing him now. He noticed, with pleased surprise, that the eyes were not blue, but amber, with dark lashes. She really was rather lovely.

She said, quite simply and naturally, "I saw you yesterday, didn't I, from the landing-stage? On your boat in the river?"

"Yes," he found himself saying, just as easily. "I saw you, too."

"It's very thick again today, isn't it?"

"Unfortunately. I wanted to get on to Lézardrieux this afternoon."

She opened her eyes very wide.

"But you won't try it, will you?"

He shook his head, smiling at her evident concern.

"My cousin tells such awful tales of the things that happen to boats among the rocks round this part of the coast," she went on, flushing a little. "But of course you know all about it."

"I've been in here twice before," he said. By this time his postcards were stamped and he had paid for the stamps and was ready to go. There was no need to talk to this girl any longer. Perhaps just a word of thanks for the use of the landing-stage.

She accepted his formal little speech gravely. This should have been the end of the conversation, but he found himself saying, "I must pick up my crew at the hard. They are on an oyster hunt."

"Oh," she said. "But they won't find any there. I mean, the fishermen bring everything up to the village. It all goes into Tréguier in a van that comes out every day. Unless you order in advance."

"Then we shan't be lucky. I'd better go down and find them and tell them so. How do I get there?"

She began to explain, and he realised that it was more complicated than he had thought, with the mist making landmarks invisible.

"It doesn't sound as if I'll find them," he said, and added, on a sudden impulse, "unless you will very kindly show me."

She looked at her watch.

"Yes," she said, with the same straightforward simplicity. "I'd like to see them again. I told Henry, that's my cousin, Henry Davenport, about them, and the boat, and he said it was quite all right about the landing-stage."

"Don't bother to come if you haven't time, Miss Davenport."

"Oh," she laughed. "I've all the time in the world, really I don't *have* to do anything. Francine, Henry's housekeeper, is too marvellous. There are maids, as well. It's unbelievable, after England. Quite feudal."

They began to walk away down the village street. When they came to the end of it and moved off along the steep cobbled road to the hard, she said, as if there had been no break in the

B

conversation. "And my name isn't Davenport, it's Brockley, Susan Brockley. Henry is my mother's nephew, though he's about twelve years older than me."

They walked down the hill out of the mist of the village into a thick all-embracing fog. Guided by Susan, there was no difficulty in finding the hard, but Giles began to wonder if his crew had found it, and in any case how he was going to find them. For though he and the girl wandered up and down the grey stones, and though they asked several of the fishermen if they had met two foreigners trying to buy shellfish, they met with no response but brief shakes of the head and muttered negatives. Only one man condescended to speak to them, and he and Giles recognised one another.

"You passed me last evening, going down the river," Giles told him, in French.

"You wanted to know if you were safe where you'd anchored. There is not much danger just there, in the *river*," the man grinned, implying a double meaning.

"I didn't want to go aground," Giles explained, wondering a little.

"One always takes the ground."

"With 'legs', yes. I have no 'legs' for my yacht. We don't need them in the English harbours."

The man grinned again, pityingly. Giles and Susan turned away.

"No good telling them we don't have thirty-foot tides on our side of the Channel," he said. "They expect to dry out here."

She did not answer and they walked back up the hill in silence.

"I seem to have missed Tony and Pip altogether," Giles said when they had walked the length of the village street, inquired at the shops, and drawn a complete blank.

"They probably gave it up and went back to the landing-stage," Susan suggested.

"More than likely. I'd better get back there, myself. In any case it's getting on for lunch time."

"I'll show you the quickest path," she said.

They went into the grounds of the château by the main gates, and along a broad drive, marked by the wheels of cars, and bordered by a generous crop of weeds. The drive led them in a wide sweep round and up the hill. Below, on their right, the mist lay thickly in what seemed to Giles to be a clearing in a hollow. He pointed it out to his companion.

"Actually it's that creek off the river," she answered. "The one that goes back from the harbour. Very shallow at low tide. Almost all a sort of muddy sand, which is supposed to be dangerous. There's a notice Henry put up, but of course the village people wouldn't think of bathing there at all. I like it, but it's rather a weird sort of place."

They went on, climbing more steeply now, but the drive had been cut into the slope, and the way was not as steep as the path Giles had used earlier. The mist was left behind again, the sun shone brightly through the overhanging trees. But not with the clear, heartening warmth he had welcomed when he came out on the road with Tony and Phillipa. The air of the drive was motionless, hot, oppressive, smelling of damp and decay. The whole approach to the house had an uncomfortable air of neglect, of effort exhausted.

They walked round another bend into a broad sweep of rough gravel. The house, half in shade, stood on the far side.

It was quite an attractive place, Giles thought. The two small conical towers, one at each end, were in the tradition of the châteaux; the warm yellow-grey stone of the walls carried on this style, though the size and general appearance of the rest of the building did not suggest any great age.

But the ubiquitous air of neglect hung over the house. Tall weeds pressed against the foot of the stone walls, filling what might have been flower beds on either side of the door. A climbing rose, unpruned for years, covered the corner of the house. Its weight had broken it away from the wall and new shoots had thrust their way into a laurel bush nearby, and were festooned across a path that led from the drive round the hidden corner. Giles noticed, with amused disgust, that a new path had been trodden in the grass round the laurel bush in order to avoid the obstructing rose.

He saw that Susan was watching him intently.

"Your cousin has a very big place to keep up," he said.

She shook her head sadly, understanding what he meant.

"He doesn't. I wish he would. But he's been so worried . . ."

Giles looked at his watch, and said quietly, "You must tell me where I go from here. Tony and Pip will be wild if I'm late for lunch. Pip has great plans for it."

"I don't think they will," Susan exclaimed, in quite a different voice. "I think they are here at the moment, talking to Henry!"

She pointed towards the house, and Giles, who was trying to find a path from the drive, turned back again. As his eyes swept the windows in turn, looking for his friends, his attention was drawn upwards by the sudden movement of a curtain. For a few seconds a face, chalk-white, staring, looked out at him. Then it was gone, leaving him breathless with shock.

It could not possibly be a face he remembered! It must be an hallucination, brought on by the irritating frustration of the fog, the queer, depressing, suspended atmosphere of the way into this place.

"Look," said Susan, who had begun to walk forward. "They're waving to you. We'd better go in."

"Where?" asked Giles. His voice was unsteady, and the girl turned to him in some surprise.

"The window beyond the door. What's the matter?"

"I saw someone upstairs—looking out."

She frowned. He was behaving very strangely. Did he not want to meet his friends again? Was something wrong on the yacht, between these three strangers? After all, she did not know them in the least; she only knew that this man was more attractive than anyone she had ever met.

"Probably Francine," she said. "The housekeeper."

As they reached the door it was opened by a stoutish, elderly woman in a neat black dress, unmistakably French, who told Susan that Mr. Henry had taken the English lady and gentleman to the library and would be pleased if they would join him there.

"Thank you, Francine," said the girl, moving ahead.

Giles followed. It had not been the stout housekeeper at the upper window. His uneasiness grew. The experience had been as new as it was shocking. For eight years he had been blotting that face from his memory, by every effort of will and reason, by every acceptance of growing disregard. He had even welcomed, this morning, the arrival on the scene of Susan Brockley. While he was persuading himself to admire her fresh looks, he had not once remembered, had not once compared her, with that earlier standard of perfection. And yet that face had appeared to him again, in an unnatural distortion, livid, horrible, and he wondered if he were going out of his mind.

Henry Davenport came forward as Susan and Giles entered the room. He was a shortish man, stockily built, but with a thin, pale face and dull eyes. A sick man, Giles thought, or an unhappy one. Perhaps both. However, Henry greeted the newcomer with some degree of warmth and turned away to supply him with a drink.

The room was low-ceilinged and panelled in dark wood. The chairs, the tables, even the books on the shelves, wore the same neglected air as the grounds outside the house. It was as if their owner had ceased to be able to see them, had failed entirely to notice their slow creeping decay. Some strange preoccupation must cause this total indifference, Giles thought. For the bearing of the French housekeeper had been brisk and alert. She did not look the sort of woman to allow slatternly habits among her staff. And yet the covers on the very English upholstered easy chairs were faded and worn, and though there was no dust on the tables, there was no polish, either.

Giles laughed to himself. He was thinking like an old hen housewife, and that was not a familiar rôle with him, confirmed bachelor though he might be. He took his glass of sherry from Henry's outstretched hand and they both moved towards the window, where Phillipa and Tony were standing, smiling at him.

"We certainly didn't expect this sort of reward for trespassing," he said, heartily, turning again to look at his host. "It's extremely good of you."

"It's a pleasure," replied Henry, quietly, and with no sign of enthusiasm. "We are very isolated here. We have few visitors, and hardly ever fellow-countrymen."

Seeing the expectant look on the three faces before him, he added, "My father came to live in this place after the First World War. He was the only male survivor of his family at the end of it. I was brought up here, but educated in England."

"Then you were over there for the second war, I suppose?"

"Oh, yes. We both were. My father got out in the winter of '39. He had no illusions about France. But the people here resented it. They thought he ought to have stayed, though what good that would have done. . . . German officers were billeted in this house. Everything went to pieces. It has never recovered. It still feels contaminated."

"Uncle George helped much more by going, Mother always says," added Susan, heartily. "Working in Intelligence, and helping to get people away from this coast. So did you, the last two years."

There was an uncomfortable silence. Giles looked at his watch again.

"We really ought to be going," he said. "We've been ashore more than two hours. And the fog was pretty thick in the river."

"It will have lifted by now," said Henry. "But I mustn't keep you if you are anxious about your yacht." His indifference was pointed by his adding, "Susan will show you the shortest path down to the river."

They wondered how he knew about the fog, if he did know. There was no view from the windows of the dark room. It ran the whole width of the house. The window in front looked out on the drive, which was surrounded by bushes. There was another big window at the back, and this showed a dank lawn of long grass, upon which the sun shone through the trees in a bright circle at one corner, while the rest lay in shade. Leafy branches, hanging low across the upper part of the window, blotted out the sky.

"How did you know the fog has gone?" Phillipa asked, impulsively.

Henry stared at her, not in resentment, but in slow surprise.

"Because that's the sort of weather it is," he said. "And will be until the wind goes back into the west."

"You mean we may be stuck here another day?" Giles asked. The indignant dismay in his voice made them all smile.

"Unless you feel confident of getting out to sea in the fog. There probably isn't any ten miles out."

"We want to go on round the coast. Lézardrieux, Isle Bréhat, eventually St. Malo."

"In that case, I expect you'll have to put up with Penguerrec. Or Tréguier, of course. You'll be able to go up the river this evening."

Giles resented his host's air of authority, but the chap must know what he was talking about. He lived here, and used the water. Giles always made it a rule to respect local knowledge of the sea and its ways. He did so now.

"Well, thanks a lot," he said. "Perhaps you'll come aboard some time, if we're staying. And Miss Brockley, of course."

"Susan might like to come up to Tréguier with us this afternoon," Phillipa suggested.

"Would you?" Giles's voice sounded quite eager.

The girl's face lit up with a radiant smile. But before she could answer, the door behind them opened, and a woman stood on the threshold.

Giles stared at her. The room span mistily about him, then cleared. It was the face he had seen at the window; the face he had hoped never to look at again. He watched her proud neck stiffen as she lifted her head to stare back at him. The high cheek bones, the long brown eyes, the black wings of hair, swept back in a fashionably careless manner now, he noticed; the wide curving mouth, the perfect skin; all, across the length of the low, dark room, exactly as he remembered them. Miriam, whom he had last seen eight years ago, taking leave of him with her usual ardent passion. Whose cool little note, two days later, told him that their impending marriage could not now take place. Miriam, whose lips were parting in her familiar smile of heart-piercing sweetness, whose eyes were lighting with a totally unexpected, unaccountable welcome.

He stepped back behind Phillipa, with a quick, total revulsion from this encounter.

"Ah," said Henry, in a bleak voice. "My wife—Mrs. Marshall, Mr. Marshall, Mr. Armitage."

CHAPTER III

THE CONVERSATION WAS general, mainly explanatory. Very slowly Giles's embarrassment faded, though his utter bewilderment and protesting incredulity remained. Miriam, of all people. The lost love turning up in the last place on earth he would have looked at, if he had been trying to find her. Peeping at him from a window of this seedy make-believe château above the river. How long had she been here? Henry Davenport was not the name that had wrecked his happiness. Or was it? He was amused to find that he really did not remember. Perhaps she had never told him. Her exit from his life, like her re-entry, had been characteristically dramatic. He was delighted to find it so utterly painless, and was both surprised and elated by his own mild cynicism.

Meanwhile the others chattered together, a lively set of variations on the theme of the persisting fog, and what it had meant to them all in terms of altered plans.

"Not that my wife and I were much put out by it," Henry said, glancing across at her, where she sat with Phillipa on a wide window seat. "We were in Paris and the car met our train at the station. My chauffeur is a Breton born and bred. He could find his way about the country roads in any weather."

"Did you have a good time in Paris?" Giles asked, feeling it was time he joined in the conversation.

Henry did not answer. But Miriam turned her head to look at him, and said, in a slow grave voice, suggesting hidden depths of sorrow, "Henry does not go to Paris for fun. He goes for treatment of his slipped disc."

There was an awkward pause. Henry, ignoring his wife's explanation, filled up his guests' glasses. Giles moved closer to Susan, who was sitting a little way from the others, only taking part in the conversation when someone spoke directly to her. She smiled up at him and then glanced out of the window.

"It's clearing," she said.

"How d'you know? There was no mist up here, earlier."

"By the clouds."

He followed her gaze and nodded.

"How right you are. The wind has gone round, too."

Henry was filling Tony's glass.

"Slipped disc?" the latter said, cheerfully. "Beastly condition. I'm sure I've got one myself. My back gives me hell at the start of every season."

"That's just stiffness," said his wife. "Hauling on ropes, and lifting weights which you never do at home."

"How does it affect you?" Tony went on, addressing Henry. "You seem pretty active. You'd need to be, living on the side of a precipice like this."

Henry smiled: a reluctant smile, Giles saw, of politeness, not amusement. He was about to answer, when Miriam said, in her slow, tense way, "Sitting at his desk, mainly. It's so important. Whatever happens, he must be able to work in comfort. He is a writer."

"Oh, I see," muttered Tony, with an Englishman's instinctive recoil from the arts. "Very inconvenient. Does it affect typing, as well?"

"I actually write in long hand," said Henry, quietly. "I am not good at typing. At present I am very lucky to have Susan here. She has been typing for me."

"Are you an expert?" Giles asked her.

"I've had some training," she answered, laughing, "but that isn't quite the same thing."

"I'm sure it is in your case."

They went on talking about her work, and Giles discovered something of her life in England. She still lived at home, in a country town, mainly looking after two rather elderly parents. They had kindly lent her to Henry for the summer, because they were themselves going on a long-planned cruise to the West Indies.

"It was lucky for me that Henry wanted me to be here," she said.

"Wouldn't you have liked the cruise?"

"Oh, yes. But they couldn't afford to take me as well. Obviously."

Obviously, Giles thought, they were a selfish pair. He was indignant to learn that they kept the girl at home, where she couldn't do more than casual jobs for pocket money, instead of letting her get on and earn enough to take herself abroad.

"I'm glad I came," she said, lowering her voice, and looking significantly at Miriam and back at Giles. "She isn't a bit well. And Francine doesn't understand her. Thinks it is just affectation. It isn't. I know it isn't."

Just affectation. Giles nodded. He found himself wishing the moment was suitable for telling Susan about himself and Miriam. And then he heard the latter's voice again, saying to Phillipa, "I wish he would go to England, and see a specialist. This Paris man is supposed to be first-rate, but the French never give me the same confidence. Do you know what I mean?"

"I have never been ill in France," said Phillipa.

"Lucky you. Henry has the most fantastic things to take, all according to an elaborate plan. I think most of it is mumbo-jumbo."

"Not entirely," said Henry. He had been showing Tony some old maps of the Brittany coast-line, which he had taken from a high shelf on the other side of the library, but he had evidently heard his wife's remark.

"Not entirely," he repeated, coming back towards the group near the window. "These new drugs, cortisone, and so on, are very up to date and they need careful handling. One is given them for a limited period at a time. The point is, they work. Temporarily, at all events."

"Francine agrees with me that it's probably all bunkum. If your disc has slipped they ought to put it back. She always says so."

"Francine is an ignorant old woman, and as superstitious as they come."

"She adores you, and she's bitterly disappointed you won't drink her own filthy concoctions."

The tone of these exchanges was light, suitably flippant, but there was an edge to both their voices that silenced all the others.

Giles made a show of looking at his watch.

"I'm afraid we really must make tracks now," he said, heartily. "There are several jobs we have to do on board before we leave this part of the river."

Phillipa jumped up, a trifle too readily, gathering together her shopping bag and the milk can.

"I must get going on my lunch," she said. "I've got the most marvellous food in here. Oysters, fillet steak, peaches."

"Come on," said Tony. "I can't wait."

They thanked their hosts and moved towards the door.

"See you this afternoon," said Giles to Susan. "We shall go up river to Tréguier on the tide about six. But come along earlier for tea. O.K?"

The girl hesitated, looking round for Miriam. But the latter was at the door, moving through it with Phillipa.

"I'll expect you," Giles urged.

"I'll come if I can," she answered. He left her standing near the window, smiling at him, the sun bright on her hair.

Giles strode rapidly ahead down the path through the woods. Behind him Tony and Phillipa were delayed by Henry, who insisted, after all, upon coming with them to the landing-stage, and who kept stopping to point out some tree or shrub worthy of notice.

Giles was impatient to get back to the seclusion of his boat. His thoughts, if not his feelings, were in turmoil. He wanted only to find some simple job to do on deck, where he could allow the peace of his surroundings to sort out and subdue the disturbance.

He was aghast, therefore, when he came round a corner of the path through the trees, to see Miriam, standing at the junction of yet another track with the main way down the hill.

"I had to speak to you, Giles," she said, breathlessly, and stood looking at him, one hand up to her neck, in a gesture he remembered only too clearly.

He felt nothing but a cold anger.

"I'm sorry we burst upon you as we did," he answered, very quietly. "Naturally, if I'd known, it would have been the last thing I'd have done."

"You haven't forgiven me—even now?"

He said, impatiently, "Really, Miriam, need we talk like a third-rate magazine? There isn't the slightest need for anything of the sort. You had a perfect right to alter your mind. Only of course it wasn't on Davenport's account. I have forgotten whose, but I'm sure his name wasn't Henry."

"You are cruel," she said, and two large tears rose in her big dark eyes. "I made a terrible mistake about George. It was George Banks. Perhaps you didn't know him. I wrote to tell you it was a mistake."

"I never had any letter."

She reddened slightly, and her eyes fell before his accusing face.

"I meant to write," she said, in a low voice.

He laughed.

"You were always a prize liar. But we needn't go into that, either. We needn't rake up any of the past. It was finished eight years ago."

"Are you married, Giles?"

He shook his head, beginning to walk on again. His anger had died, but he longed to finish this unprofitable conversation. He went on, but he could hear Miriam, on the narrow path behind him, following in his footsteps. When he reached the landing-stage he paused, waiting for the others. Miriam stood still, watching him.

Without meaning to, he went on where they had left off.

"Never mind about me," he said. "The point is you married this chap, Davenport, and you have a fine house, and—and——"

"And I have nothing to complain of?" said Miriam. "Is that what you mean?"

"Well, I'm right, aren't I?"

The eyes widened. He felt, against reason, against outraged

pride, the old surge of anxious distress for her predicament. Her palpable anxiety flooded into his own being, though he fought against it with all his maturer self.

"I am afraid," she whispered.

Giles stared at her. She had always exaggerated: she was a prize liar, she loved, and lived for, sensation, however childishly contrived. But in spite of his knowledge of her, his reviving painful memories, he could not help being impressed.

In an impulse to escape from the situation he had begun to move along the landing-stage, level now, as the water had only just begun to go down.

"Help me, Giles," she went on, her voice rising. "You must help me!"

He had to look back at her. He was too far away to speak comforting words. He could not shout them. It was a ridiculous position; he wanted to laugh, but he could not. That white face, those terrified eyes, stopped mirth. Liar she might be, but there always was, there always had been, he corrected himself, some background to her fantasies. So he walked back again, and stood over her.

"What exactly do you mean?" he asked, in a voice loaded with contempt and unbelief.

Miriam lifted her hand, listening.

"The others," she said. "Another time." She added, in a rapid undertone, looking up at him, "You aren't really angry with me, are you, Giles? It seemed a miracle when I saw you from the window. I thought I was saved. I need help. I do need help. You must believe me."

He did not believe her, but again he felt the dread chill of her anguish, which was real, however imaginary its cause. He had to protect himself against it.

"I'm sorry if you are upset over something," he said, tritely. "I don't expect it's as bad as you think. But I'm not much use to you, I'm afraid. We are going up river after tea, and on to Lézardrieux tomorrow."

The rest of the party joined them on the stage. Tony and Phillipa exclaimed in delight at finding the mist entirely gone. Giles was amazed. He had been there for over ten minutes and had not even noticed this simple fact. Miriam had so imposed herself and her mysterious problem upon him that he had been for those minutes quite oblivious of his surroundings. It was uncanny. It was also humiliating and dangerous.

"I wouldn't trust it," Henry said. "When the fog goes suddenly like this with a change of wind, it usually means bad weather coming in from the Atlantic."

"It cleared yesterday," said Tony, "in the afternoon. Just like this."

"The forecast wasn't too bright this morning, though," Giles reminded him. "It mentioned a depression. And the glass had gone down several pips when we came ashore."

Henry was looking down river, towards the hard.

"I see they are making their boats fast to the wall," he said. "That means they are expecting a blow. They will not be going out today, even now it has cleared."

"*Bad* weather?" said Phillipa, incredulously, looking round at the summer scene.

"Well, we'd better get back on board," Giles said, briskly. "Get the next shipping forecast at one-forty."

They all said goodbye to the Davenports, thanked them for their hospitality, and went out along the stage. Giles called back, "Don't let Susan be late. We want to start up river between five and six."

Seeing blank faces he explained, "She's coming along for the trip up to Tréguier."

Henry nodded and turned away, but Miriam moved towards the dinghy.

"She must have forgotten," she said, slowly and distinctly. "She promised to drive me to Paimpol this afternoon. I don't drive, unfortunately. I'm afraid she won't be able to come."

"She *promised* to come!" Giles spoke with a boyish emphasis that made Phillipa smile.

"What a pity," Miriam answered. Then, with a smile and a wave of her hand she followed her husband into the shelter of the trees.

"Damnation!" said Giles. On the way out to *Shuna* in the dinghy he did not speak another word.

Clouds blew up from the west during the afternoon, putting out the sun. The forecast had been depressing; the fine weather was leaving them. Tony and Phillipa waited for the skipper's word to go up river, but he spent the time on deck, morose and silent, and tea came and went, and still no orders were given.

"I'll have to think about what to make for dinner, if we go on waiting," suggested Phillipa.

"If we're waiting for Susan to show up, Giles will be disappointed. Mrs. Davenport was about as likely to part with her as a steel trap."

"She's a queer creature," said Phillipa. "Odd her turning up at the landing-stage with Giles. She must have beetled down another of their forest paths. On purpose to have him to herself, do you think?"

"Stop building scandal. I'll get the skipper down for a conference."

Giles went below reluctantly. He still hoped that Susan would come, but he knew that it was an unreasonable hope. Miriam had decided that. She was not going to let the girl enjoy a trip she was not herself invited to share. That was the old Miriam; the selfish, self-absorbed Miriam, who must be at the centre of every project. She had not changed at all, it seemed, in her desires. But was her power undimmed? Could she still impose her will on everyone about her, as she had done in the old days? Was Susan not young enough, and independent enough, in a matter-of-fact, take it for granted, modern fashion, to withstand the emotional tyranny of her cousin's wife? Or would she submit meekly, agree to drive Miriam to Paimpol? A false engagement, surely, invented on the spot, or the girl would have told him of it when he asked her to join them on *Shuna*.

While they discussed what they ought to do, Giles kept going up on deck to see if Susan had arrived on the landing-stage. The tide was coming up again now, but the ladders were still exposed. The mud smelt of stale fish. And no one came there, down the path through the trees. Another hour went by and another. The Marshalls waited patiently, but Phillipa peeled some potatoes and reviewed her larder. Giles went on deck and stayed there.

"Something's happened to him," Phillipa said to her husband.

"Several things, seemingly," Tony agreed.

"He was knocked flat by Susan, for a start. Or as flat as he ever is, which means practically vertical."

"He'd obviously met Mrs. Davenport before. Extraordinary woman, didn't you think?"

"We agreed on that. It's all rather upsetting. I mean the atmosphere in that house. Susan's Cousin Henry gave me the creeps. So very affable, and really not there at all. It was like talking to a sleep-walker."

"Don't work it up. Everything was all right until the wife came into the room and the buzzer went off between her and Giles. Incidentally Henry must have noticed. Perhaps that accounts for him being so detached afterwards."

"Why don't you get Giles to tell you about it? Do him a power of good. And it might clear the air for him over Susan. I have a feeling that particular angle ought to be encouraged."

"You would," said her husband. But he took her advice and joined Giles on deck. The latter began to give several very lame excuses for not going up to Tréguier that evening, the chief of them being that they had left it too late to have dinner there. Tony listened in silence and did not hide the fact that he found these explanations unnecessary. He tried to lead the conversation to the Davenports, but Giles was not drawn, and his friend failed to get any interesting details of his more remote past. He knew that Giles was often attracted to women and always professed to despise them. He realised now that his and Phillipa's cheerful curiosity was out of place. The whole thing must be much more serious than they suspected.

He managed to convey this to her before Giles finally joined them below for dinner. She was suitably impressed. The light-hearted holiday mood of the morning had vanished. And their surroundings had changed, too. The mist had not come back, but neither had the sun. The grey sky had turned the trees to a dull heavy midsummer green. The harbour wall and the

34 *The House Above the River*

cottages at Penguerrec were a harsh grey in the evening light. The wind had begun to sing in the rigging, and even where they lay in the river, little white-capped waves, whipped up by it, slapped at *Shuna*'s topsides. The shipping forecast had given gale warnings for the whole length of the Channel.

CHAPTER IV

THE WIND BLEW harder and harder all night, and by morning
Shuna was rocking on a heavy swell, rolling in from the
sea.

Giles woke early, after a night of many disturbances. Both he
and Tony had been up on deck several times in the dark hours,
trying to locate and subdue some of the many noises produced
by flapping ends of rope and rattling blocks. Even the soft,
rubber-protected bump of the dinghy, tied fore and aft alongside, was maddening when endlessly repeated. After he could
bear it no longer, Giles went up again, to alter the fenders and
secure the warps more tightly. Then he wriggled into his sleep-
ing-bag once more, to drowse fitfully until the grey morning
light brought the day at last.

By now the gale was at its height. The three listened in a
gloomy silence to the shipping forecast. It gave them no hope
of better things for the next twenty-four hours at least. They
got up and dressed, and Phillipa made breakfast, surprised to
find she was less upset by the movement of the boat now than
she had been on the way over from England.

"Sea legs coming along nicely, Pip." Giles congratulated
her. "Bouncing about at anchor, like this, is the ultimate
test."

"I'm fine, so far."

Giles put his head and shoulders out into the cockpit. There
was a choppy little sea all round them. Near the hard at Penguerrec the whole surface of the water was white with spray,
while further off, on the other side of the river, he could see
great waves breaking over the rocks at Pen Paluch.

"It would probably be more comfortable further up the
river," he said. "And I dare say we could get the anchor up
without being blown on the mud. If you're both fed up
with hanging about here so long, I'm quite willing to
move."

"Personally," said Tony, "I'd rather stay put. You told us yourself it was practically impossible to get ashore at Tréguier at low tide. Here we don't have to worry."

"Fair enough." On the whole Giles seemed pleased. "Will that suit you, Pip?"

"Yes. Particularly as it's now beginning to rain, and I don't see any fun in standing out in the cockpit, motoring, with water dripping down my neck."

"How right you are."

Giles retreated into the cabin, pulling the hatch shut as he did so. The rain, driven by the high wind, beat down on *Shuna*'s decks, and against her portholes. Giles moved about below, looking for drips.

"Wonderfully dry boat," he said, complacently. Tony, who was lying on a bunk, with his feet up, reading, winced as a cold drop hit the top of his head.

"Marvellous," he said, getting out a handkerchief to mop the spot. He looked up to discover the leak, and received the next drop in his right eye.

"One small drip!" said Giles, indignantly. "I don't think there's much to complain of in that."

"I haven't complained."

"Only suffered obviously, which is worse," said his wife. "Move up, and let me investigate."

Tony took his book to the opposite bunk.

"It's stopping," said Phillipa. "The rain, I mean. Not the wind."

"Yes. I'm afraid the wind is winning at present."

"What's that?" she said, presently.

"What's what?"

"Someone hailing us, I think."

Giles pulled the cover of the hatch back a few inches and a cascade of water fell down the companion-way. He swore heartily. A shout, distinctly heard by all three of them, cut across the singing of the wind.

"It's your new girl-friend, old boy," said Tony, lazily. "Nice day for a stroll in the woods."

But Giles was up on deck by now and did not hear him.

Susan was on the landing-stage in a mackintosh coat and hat, and gumboots.

"Hello!" Giles called to her. "What are you doing out on a filthy morning like this?"

She laughed and caught at the ladder of the stage to steady herself.

"Can you hear me?" she called.

"Just about."

"We want you to come up to the house till the storm blows out."

"To *stay*, do you mean?"

"Yes. Henry says it'll be two days, at least, before you can move."

Giles went along the deck towards the dinghy, remembered he had not got oilskins on, and stopped.

"Look," he shouted. "I'll come across and bring you off here, and we'll talk it over."

The girl nodded. This was what she had hoped for, having been prevented from seeing *Shuna* the day before.

Giles went below. The rain was nearly over, for the time being, and he had not got very wet. He put on oilskins and sea boots, and took the dinghy rowlocks off the shelf.

"Want any help?" Tony asked, not moving. Giles made a face at him.

"I'll brew some coffee," said Phillipa. "What does she want, Giles? The visit Mrs. D. baulked her of?"

"By no means. It's an invitation to stay at the château."

"Is it, indeed?"

But Giles had gone, without answering, and they heard him untying the dinghy, and setting off for the shore.

Susan stood waiting on the stage. She admired the easy way he handled the little boat in the choppy waves of the river. She hoped she would not make any terrible mistakes getting into it, herself. She had no qualms about the trip out to the yacht. Giles was far too competent for that.

With his quiet advice, and the help of a strong hand, she got down into the dinghy neatly, and instinctively, though she knew nothing of boats, settled herself in the centre of the thwart to balance it. Giles noted this with satisfaction. On the rather wet row against the wind and the waves, back to *Shuna*, he admired still further her complete serenity.

"Sorry about this," he said, as a wave hit the bows of the dinghy and spray flew over them both. "I ought to have warned you, perhaps."

"Much better not," she laughed. "Or I mightn't have come."

"I don't believe it."

They both laughed, and neither felt that rain or spray or any other discomfort counted at all beside the pleasure of being there together.

The house, that had seemed so gloomy and forbidding on the sunny day of their first visit, now appeared in a much more welcoming guise. Compared with the general discomfort of a yacht at anchor in a gale of wind and rain, they found dry warmth, and room to stretch their legs, and a firm surface under their feet, most heartening.

When they arrived, Susan told them to dump their bags in the hall, and then led them to a small, pleasantly furnished sitting-room, where a log fire, recently lit, crackled on the hearth.

"This is Miriam's room," the girl explained. "I thought she'd be here. I'll go and find her while you thaw out."

The three friends waited in silence. Phillipa sat down to warm her hands, cold from the rain; Tony got out a pipe and filled it, but put it back in his pocket unlighted; Giles wandered about the room uneasily, wishing he had not come. When the door opened, they all started. But it was only Francine, in her neat black dress, covered now with a small flowered apron.

After greeting them all politely, she said, in her precise, high-pitched French voice, "Would you like me to show you to your rooms?"

She spoke with the slight burr of a Breton accent, reminding Giles of the English west-country dialects. Her French, however, was perfectly intelligible to all of them.

They followed her up a wide staircase, along a passage and round a corner into a short corridor, with a window at the end.

She opened two doors, on either side of this corridor, waving the Marshalls towards one, and Giles towards the other. They separated and went into their respective rooms.

Giles noticed at once that his bag was there already, placed on a chair under the window. This room, being further from ground level than those he had already seen, was less shut in by the trees, though the view was equally restricted to the woods that closed upon the house from all sides. While he was still looking out of the window, he heard the door of the room close behind him, and turning, saw Francine, standing just inside it, her hands clasped over her apron.

"Monsieur must forgive me," she said, "if I speak to him about Madame."

"Which Madame?" he asked, smiling, and wondering what on earth she meant.

"Madame Davenport."

He frowned, and was about to refuse to listen to her, when she came forward a few steps, and went on in a hurried, pleading manner that quite astonished him.

"Madame is ill. She has been ill for many years. Here, you understand." She tapped her forehead significantly. "Everyone is afraid for her, and a little afraid of her, too. Now Monsieur has arrived, so unexpectedly, and it has had a most profound effect on Madame. The depression is gone, but she is over-excited, she seems to be in a fever. We have had these crises before, but this is worse than any."

"What has it all to do with me?" asked Giles, steadily.

Francine drew herself up. She said, with great dignity and respect, "It is quite clear to us all that you are a very old friend of Madame."

"Did she tell you that, herself?"

"Of course not. Monsieur Davenport told me. He must have learned it from Madame."

"Monsieur Davenport talks to you about his private affairs?"

She smiled.

"I have known him since he was a little boy, tearing his clothes in the woods, getting them wet in the fishermen's boats."

"I see." He thought for a moment, then said, gravely, "It is quite true that I used to know Madame Davenport. But I have not seen her for eight years. I did not know whom she had married; I did not know she was living here. If I had known it," he finished, with slow emphasis on every precise French word he used, "I should not have come into the house."

Francine met his eyes with a gaze as frank and serious as his own. But she only said, as at length she turned to open the door, "You speak very good French, monsieur. You have no accent at all."

"I spent my war in the British Navy," he answered, "and that included the west coast of France, North Africa, and later Normandy. Also I come to your side of the Channel nearly every summer in my yacht. I have been to Tréguier twice before!"

"But you have never visited us till now."

"I never even knew there was a house above the river. I never noticed the landing-stage till it appeared out of the fog."

Francine sighed. As she opened the door she said, in a low voice, "It would be better that Madame did not know I have spoken to you like this."

Giles answered, "May I remind you that I am not in Madame's confidence?"

He hoped the old busybody would understand from his tone of voice that he did not want to be in Madame's confidence, and would damn well see he was not exposed to it. Watching Francine's set face as she left the room he thought he had succeeded.

Meanwhile Tony and Phillipa, finding their bags also set out on chairs, had unpacked the simple contents quickly, and Phillipa had changed her slacks for a skirt. They went back to the sitting-room downstairs. This time Miriam was there, full of apologies for not having been in time to greet them when they first arrived.

"I'm afraid I get up very late," she explained.

There seemed to be no suitable answer to this. But Miriam evidently did not expect one. She went on at once to ask them about their voyage over from England, their friendship with Giles, their home surroundings and his.

"How lucky for you to have grandparents for your children, who will look after them when you go away."

Phillipa agreed warmly.

"Giles seems to have no family?"

"Oh, no, he isn't married," Tony said, and added, "In the six years we've known him he hasn't taken more than a passing interest in any of the nice girls we keep throwing at his head."

Phillipa laughed, but Miriam said, in a husky voice, "He was not always like that."

"You know him, don't you?" Phillipa asked, boldly. She was determined to clear up the implied mystery.

"I nearly married him. Eight years ago," answered Miriam, enjoying the effect of this speech.

"I'm so sorry. I wouldn't have said . . ."

"You need not be sorry! Giles is not sorry. Anyone can see that!"

The Marshalls felt very uncomfortable at this outburst. Miriam laughed, rather wildly. "I am obviously not sorry," she declared, looking from one to the other. "He walked out on me, but Henry walked in. So who is the loser?"

Tony and Phillipa exchanged glances. The woman was quite terrible, their looks conveyed. Why didn't Giles come, or Susan, to relieve them of their embarrassment?

Miriam seemed to realise the unfavourable reaction in her audience. She stooped to put another log on the fire. When she sat back again, her expression and manner were quite different.

"So you two and Giles live in the same part of the world," she said. "When I knew him he had just left the Navy, and was looking for a civilian engineering job."

"He came to my firm six years ago," Tony explained. "He's done very well. Full of ideas outside the routine jobs. In fact he invented a most useful gadget a few years ago, and patented it."

"And does very nicely out of it, bless him," said Phillipa. "This present boat of his came out of the proceeds. Much superior to the one he had when we first knew him."

Miriam was eager to hear more of Giles's prosperity. So

eager that Tony quickly changed the subject, and was relieved
a few minutes later when Giles and Susan came into the room
together, and the conversation turned inevitably to the weather
and its prospects.

Henry did not appear at luncheon. He sent a message by
Francine, begging to be excused. He was working, she explained, and would have a tray in the library.

"Henry writes," said Miriam, slowly, when Francine had
delivered her message and gone away, "Nothing is ever published. But he writes. Perhaps a great book will emerge some
day. I don't know."

"What sort of things does he write?" asked Phillipa, genuinely interested.

Miriam shrugged her shoulders, but Susan answered for her.

"Stories," she said. "Fiction, I suppose, but most of them
are war stories, and I expect they are founded on fact. And it
isn't true that they are never published. They come out quite
often in magazines."

"I meant books," said Miriam, and the subject languished.

The rain stopped during the afternoon. Giles, still feeling
restless and frustrated, proposed a walk. Miriam exclaimed in
horror at the idea, but when Susan welcomed it enthusiasti-
cally, she looked annoyed and said she supposed she had better
take some exercise. However, when it came to the point of
leaving the fireside and dressing up for the rigours of mud
underfoot and a tearing wind, she changed her mind, laughing-
ly stretching out a graceful hand towards a book on a table
nearby.

Giles felt more kindly disposed towards her at that moment
than at any time since her unwelcome reappearance. He put out
his own hand to give her the book. Their fingers touched. In
spite of a furious resentment something of her old power swept
through him. He found himself looking deep into her dark eyes:
it was difficult to take his hand away.

"I think I must write some letters," he heard Phillipa say, in
a dry voice, and realised, with a sense of shock, that they had
all been watching him.

The walk with Susan was not a success. They covered some four miles, going briskly along uneven muddy lanes between hedges. Occasionally there was a distant view of the sea, savage, white-capped waves hurling themselves against rocks in a smother of flying spray. But most of the time it was hidden behind tall hedges with round-backed fields beyond.

They passed a group of men cutting the grass at the verge. There were eight of them, in loose blue blouses and jeans, with black tight-fitting berets on their heads, and wooden sabots on their feet. They worked with scythes and billhooks and long wooden-toothed rakes of ancient design. Giles thought of the modern tractor-driven rotor scythes used on the verges of English roads, one man driving, covering miles in a day. The Bretons might be living in another age, in another world altogether. But they seemed contented enough, exchanging their occasional remarks as they moved slowly forward. He made a mild joke about their slow progress, but Susan did not respond.

So what, thought Giles, glancing at her stern profile. Let her mind her own business, he thought, rudely, only too conscious of her obvious reaction to his unexpected moment of intimacy with Miriam. He wanted very badly at that moment to tell her about Miriam. If she had not taken up this silly, school-girl attitude, he would have done so. But not now. She could think what nonsense she liked.

They parted in the hall of the house with the briefest of mutual thanks. Susan went up to her room, and Giles, after leaving his sea boots and oilskin jacket in a cupboard for such things built into the side of the dark hall, went back to Miriam's sitting-room, where he expected to find his friends.

They were not there; only Miriam herself, who put down her book, and rose to her feet as he shut the door.

"I hoped you might come alone," she said, in a low, tense voice, that roused his instant opposition. "I hoped and prayed for it."

He stood still, at a distance from her, cursing his luck. It was Susan's fault, of course. If she hadn't been such a clot, they would have come here together. Now he was in for a scene. He knew the drill. She was working herself up to it, grand drama, about the fatal misunderstanding that had parted them. Her self-deception was boundless. Or did she know she was playing a part? He felt slightly sick, and bored, unutterably bored. Miriam was the eternal adolescent, he found himself thinking, but he was now eight years older. Physical contact had disturbed him, but this sort of thing, however intensely put on, made no impression at all.

He prepared to resist the coming flood of explanation and reproach. But instead his complacency was shaken by her next words.

"Giles, you must help me! I told you I was afraid. Now I am *terrified!*"

He stared at her. Against his will he found himself moving forward until he stood on the hearthrug near her. She put a hand against his coat and again he could not move away.

"I have not been happy here, Giles. Henry has never loved me. We live quite apart, and alone. We hardly ever go away. Our visits to Paris are spent seeing doctors about his spine."

He gave a short laugh at this, and moved away at last; her hand dropped to her side.

"You are angry. You jeer. You don't want to hear about my life, do you? You used to live for every moment of it."

That touched his strong sense of the ridiculous. He laughed again.

"Really, Miriam! It's hardly decent to talk like this. Straight out of the lowest type of melodrama."

Tears stood in her eyes.

"You laugh. Go on laughing! But if I tell you I am in real danger?"

"What danger, for heaven's sake?"

She drew close again, lowering her voice.

"I swear I am in danger. It may sound impossible, but it is true. Why did Henry ask his cousin to come here?"

"To be with you, I was told," Giles said, in a surprised voice.

"*To be with him!* I live here in the house with them, and I know. Henry is working out a scheme against me, because of Susan."

"You mean he wants to divorce you, or get you to divorce him?"

"Worse than that. He wants to kill me!"

Giles remembered what Francine had told him. Perhaps the old woman was right. For there was nothing whatever of the villain about poor Henry. A quiet, rather dull, rather ill man.

"You're imagining things," he said.

"I'm not. Do you think I haven't watched them together? Do you think I haven't seen the deadly change in Henry? Perhaps he is mad, because he suffers so much pain, and because his writing is so unsuccessful. But I know I am in danger. Terrible danger. You must help me Giles! If you ever loved me, and I know you did, *you must help me now!*"

To stop her flow of words, her high-pitched, sickening, false self-dramatisation, he put his hands on her shoulders to shake the mounting hysteria out of her.

Over her head he saw Susan, standing framed in the doorway of the room.

CHAPTER V

HENRY APPEARED AT dinner that evening, in a more forth-coming mood, apparently, than on the day before. He apologised for avoiding his guests earlier in the day, explaining that when he started work he found it difficult to break off. Giles agreed with him. His own work was largely creative, and though he knew very little of the processes of art, he was reasonably well-informed and well-read. The new conversation at the meal reached a far more interesting level than that in the library had done. Only Susan and Miriam took no active part in it. The former was rather too obviously avoiding any contact with Giles. The latter was equally obviously put out by losing her place at the centre of notice.

"You are very silent, Susan," she said, presently, cutting across the general talk. "Your walk doesn't seem to have done you good. I hope you have not caught a chill."

"I enjoyed the walk," answered Susan, without enthusiasm, "and I never catch chills."

"I'm sure I shall," replied Miriam, "if we go on having arctic conditions, in August."

"It seems to us marvellously warm in the house," said Phillipa, hoping to check a further list of complaints. "You should try a wet day on the yacht."

"God forbid!" Miriam exclaimed, too loudly.

"I certainly should," Giles broke in. "I've had too many passengers on board in my time, hating every minute of it, and wishing they hadn't imagined they were born seamen."

Miriam had attained her object. She had broken Henry's short ascendancy, and she had turned all the attention to her-self. Both Phillipa and Susan, watching their host, saw the quick flash of anger in his pale eyes. Afterwards he sank again into apathy. The meal continued, with desultory conversation among the women. None of the men said much.

When they had finished breakfast the next day, Giles proposed to his crew that they should visit Tréguier that morning,
have lunch there, see the cathedral, do their shopping, and stay
away from the house until the afternoon.

Tony and Phillipa understood his predicament. He wanted
to avoid Miriam, and he had somehow fallen foul of
Susan.

"Because she thinks he's been knocked all of a heap again by
Miriam's fatal charms," Phillipa told her husband, when Giles
had left them. "Obvious situation. Silly misunderstanding.
Giles will probably let the whole thing slide. I wonder what
there really was between them? I mean, what parted them?"

"Between Susan and Giles?"

"No, darling. Don't be so dim. Between Miriam and Giles.
We shall never know. He'll never tell us, and she would only
tell lies."

"You don't have a very exalted idea of our hostess."

"I think she's a prize-winning bitch."

"Possibly. She's a damned attractive woman "

"Tony! You *can't* mean that!"

"Oh, yes, I can."

Phillipa went off to her room to get ready for the day's out-
ing. There was a bus, Giles had said, from outside the post
office in Penguerrec. They must leave in ten minutes if they
wanted to catch it.

In the Marshalls' bedroom, Francine and one of the maids
were making the bed. They finished it quickly and the girl went
away, but the old woman moved to the door and shut it.

"I would like to speak to Madame," she said, gravely.

"Oh, yes? I have to catch a bus. I am late already," answered
Phillipa, in her rather halting French.

"Madame understands what I say?"

"Yes, yes."

Phillipa put the finishing touches to her make-up, and began
going through the contents of her handbag.

"I will not keep Madame a moment," said Francine. "Only
to say that Monsieur Armitage upsets Madame Davenport.
That makes Monsieur Henri very unhappy."

Phillipa was suddenly furious. What right had this woman to say such things? To criticise Giles, of all people.

"Monsieur Armitage had no idea he would meet Madame Davenport here," she said, indignantly. Her instinct had been to say nothing, but Francine was impressive. She was not someone to be ignored. And Giles had told them she had been with Henry since his childhood.

"I wonder," said Francine, calmly, "if that can be true."

Phillipa snatched up her bag and made for the door, but Francine's solid figure stood there, blocking her path. As she came up to her the old woman put her hand into the large pocket of her apron and pulled out a folded leather photograph frame. She opened it and turned it towards Phillipa.

"Madame keeps this in her room," she said.

Phillipa pushed it away.

"Then put it back there!" she protested. There was much more she wanted to add, but her French was not equal to it.

"Let me pass," she said, fiercely, instead.

Francine made way for her. She watched her hurry away down the passage. Then she looked again at the photograph in her hand. A younger Giles, a younger Miriam, faced one another from the two sides of the case. Francine closed it and put it back in her pocket.

"What a pity," she said to herself, "that they did not marry."

The visit to Tréguier gave the party from *Shuna* much-needed relief. In spite of the gale, now beginning to blow out, they enjoyed it in the holiday spirit befitting a cruise abroad. Giles was disappointed that their meal had to be eaten inside the hotel, instead of under a gaily-striped umbrella among the magnificent hydrangeas. But the food was as good as ever, and it was largely on account of the food, he explained, that he brought his boat to France so often. They went back to Penguerrec on the bus feeling refreshed and happy.

Susan was in the hall when they got back. In his present confident mood Giles decided on the spot to settle their difference.

"Haven't you been out today?" he called to her as she turned, after greeting them, to go upstairs.

"No. Miriam needed me."

"But you're free now, aren't you?"

"I think she's asleep. She had a very bad night."

"Then you need some air, and I need some exercise after sitting in that bus, and eating a colossal meal. Get your things on and come down to the river to see if *Shuna* is all right."

"Why wouldn't she be?"

"Don't argue, girl. Skipper's orders."

She gave him a brief smile, and began to rummage in the big cupboard in the hall.

"Bother," she said, flapping through the coats that hung there. "My mac must be upstairs."

"Borrow. There are hundreds available."

"I don't think Miriam would mind if I wore hers. She won't be going out."

She pulled on gumboots and the mackintosh and joined him at the door.

They walked away from the house in silence, taking the main path into the woods. Giles had made up his mind. He would end the nonsense, here and now.

"Eight years ago," he said, looking straight ahead down the path, "I was engaged to Miriam. She wrote to me a fortnight before the wedding to say it was off. I couldn't believe it, at first. I knew she liked making scenes, but they had always ended happily. They never lasted long. This time there was no scene. She refused to see me."

"Oh, no!"

"What d'you mean, oh, no? That she didn't behave like that? Or that you don't believe any of it?"

"Neither. Miriam told me this morning that you had been engaged, but *you* broke it off, and had been sorry ever since."

Giles swore fiercely.

"You believed her?"

"I didn't know what to believe. She . . . you . . ."

"You are thinking of yesterday. When you came into the room. Do you know what I was about to do?"

Susan reddened.

"I was not going to kiss her, you little clot; I was going to

D

shake the hysteria out of her, if I shook her head off."

Susan exploded into laughter: Giles joined in, and for some
seconds neither could speak.

"Seriously, though," said Giles, at last, with an effort, "I
swear it happened as I've said; eight years ago, I mean. It
amazes me now to think I didn't see the snags at that time.
They stick out a mile. I suppose she really isn't quite normal."

"Poor thing," said Susan, also recovering her gravity. "She
seems to exist by making herself miserable."

She paused, and then asked shyly, "Did you really not know
she lived here?"

"Certainly not. Why do you think I might have known?"

"Henry thinks you did. He thinks Miriam asked you to
come."

"Good God! Did he tell you so?"

"Yes."

"I see."

He wondered if he were seeing too much. Miriam had hinted
at a close relationship between this girl and her cousin. All the
more reason for discarding such a suggestion.

"He is wrong," he exploded. "You are all wrong. Milling
about these caves of suspicion and suggestion and beastliness!
I swear she was the last person I expected, or wanted, to see. I
wish I'd gone into Lézardrieux, instead of this place. I would
have, if the wind hadn't been just right for coming here."

"Poor Giles," she said, not teasing him, but with full adult
understanding.

"Susan!"

He took her hand and held it, and they walked on together,
not speaking until they came out of the trees and saw the river
below them, and *Shuna*, swinging up and down on a heavy
swell, but lying safe to her anchor, with the ebb rushing past
her.

"She doesn't give a damn," said Giles, proudly, and Susan,
with an unreasonable pang of jealousy, knew there would always be two women in his life, and one was *Shuna*.

He dropped Susan's hand and went forward to the top of the
stage, looking up and down the river.

"The dinghy seems to be bumping your launch a bit," he said. "I'll slip down and fix it."

"Do you want any help?"

"Probably not. But come down if you like. The ladder's as slippery as hell, and stinks of river mud and fish, but not to worry."

He went down rapidly to the lowest stage, while Susan followed, moving rather clumsily in her rubber boots, because they tended to slip on the iron rungs. Giles did not wait to help her. He seemed to take it for granted she could look after herself.

"Does Henry go out much in the launch?" he asked, as Susan joined him.

"When the weather is good, yes. We've been for several trips since I've been here. He likes fishing, which I find rather boring. But there's plenty of excitement otherwise."

"How?"

"He knows all the little channels between the rocks. He was brought up here, apart from school."

"I know." Giles thought of his own scared entry down the main channel, and laughed. "That's why he wasn't much impressed by our coming in in the fog. He could do it himself, blindfold, I suppose?"

"I expect so," Susan agreed, and added, "I don't like the launch much, anyhow. I'd rather sail."

"Do you sail?"

"No. But I want to."

"You'd better come round to Lézardrieux with us, when we do manage to get off."

"I'd love to," she said, eagerly. But as they turned from the boats to go back up the stage, she said sadly, "I expect Miriam would find some excuse to stop me, though."

"To hell with Miriam!"

"It never works out like that. She brings the hell to you."

"How right you are."

On the way up the hill, Giles stopped, pointing to a narrower track on the left.

"This was where Miriam waylaid me," he said. "Is it a short cut?"

"Yes, in a way," Susan answered.

"What do you mean?"

"Well, it is actually shorter, but it brings you out at a door in the old stable wall, and unless you have the key, you have to walk right round the wall to the front of the house."

"I see. There is only one key?"

"I don't know that. But I haven't got one."

"Let's go up it, anyway. I like exploring."

"Actually, it's Miriam's favourite path in the woods. There is a clearing with a seat and a view. The seat is a sort of war memorial, to the local resistance movement. The Germans had officers billeted in the château. They disappeared from time to time, I believe. And then local people were taken and shot."

"Even in Penguerrec?"

"Everywhere, wasn't it?"

They turned into the path and walked up, in single file, Susan leading.

The clearing, as a beauty spot, Giles found disappointing. It was much overgrown with rank grass; the view, through a gap in the trees, of the distant village of Pen Paluch was restricted. Moreover, the seat was not well placed to enjoy it, for it faced down, instead of across, the clearing. He also noticed that the seat was slightly tilted, for one of the flat iron rings, like feet, that stuck out from its base at either side, was raised from the ground. He pointed all this out to Susan, as they stood at the edge of the grass, looking about them.

"I never noticed that," she said. "I think I've been here only once. Henry showed it to me soon after I came. He told me it was a favourite haunt of Miriam's. She never talks about things like that, herself."

"Far too ordinary," said Giles.

She looked at him, puzzled and sad.

"You almost hate her now, don't you?"

"No," he answered, turning his face away from her. "No. Myself. For wasting so many years on a sentimental memory. For not letting myself grow out of it. Till now."

Turning to her, he saw her eyes fill with tears.

"Darling," he said, under his breath.

Before Susan could recover from the surprise of this address, they were both roused by a voice calling to them from the opposite side of the clearing. They turned their heads quickly, and saw Henry, standing among the trees.

"We've been down to look at *Shuna*," Giles shouted, cheerfully, while Susan started to walk, almost to run, across the grass.

It happened without any kind of warning. Giles saw the girl hurry on to a rough patch of ground, covered with broken branches. He saw her stumble, beginning to fall forward. He heard her terrified shout as the ground gave way under her feet. And then, even while she was disappearing from view, he leaped forward.

From where he had been standing he could not now have seen her, but he covered the space between them in a few seconds, and saw her mackintoshed arm, thrown across one log stouter than the rest, which had its ends firmly fixed on either side of a great hole in the ground.

He flung himself down beside the gap, wondering if his added weight would take them both into whatever depths lay beneath. He reached for her arm, and took it in a firm grip at the wrist. Down the hole he saw her white face lose its look of mad terror.

"I've got you," he said. "But I don't know how firm it is where I am. Can you bring your other hand up?"

Without speaking, she did so, and he grasped that wrist, too, in his free hand. Then he began to wriggle slowly backwards, drawing her to the edge of the hole.

"You'll have to let go the log," he ordered, when progress stopped.

"No. Half a minute." Her voice was faint, but resolute. "I think I can get my foot on the rock."

"Rock?"

"Yes. It's rock all round me. There's hardly any earth. Can you give me a pull? A hard one?"

"No. I'm the wrong way round. I daren't try to get up."

"All right. Just hold on, and I'll do the pulling. Let me have my right hand."

Unwillingly he began to shift his grip, but he felt her fingers close on his arm with a firm clasp. A second later she came up out of the hole. He let go her other wrist to grasp at her shoulder, and she fell forward on top of him.

For a few moments they lay still, panting. Then Giles freed himself, got up and lifted her to her feet. She did not faint or cry, only stood, leaning against him, shivering.

"We must get back to the house," he said, gently, but did not take away his supporting arms.

"Henry. What happened to Henry?" was all she managed to say. And then, "My teeth won't stop chattering."

Henry. Giles had forgotten him. What had the blighter been doing, not to help them? He had been standing there, on the other side of the clearing. He must have seen Susan fall. But he had vanished. He had not helped. He had just gone away.

And then Giles saw him, in company with another man, running from the direction of the château. They carried a long coil of rope between them.

"Don't hurry!" Giles called to him. The sharp sarcasm in his voice brought Henry to a dead stop. He came on again slowly. As he drew close, Susan lifted her head, but she did not move, and Giles still held her close.

"I didn't go right down, Henry," she said. "Giles got me out."

There was a dull note in her voice that Giles did not like. She must have suffered more shock than she was showing at present.

"You seem to have had a landslide or something," he said to Henry. "The rain, perhaps."

"No." Henry seemed to have some difficulty in speaking. The other man, in a blue labourer's blouse, said nothing.

"What d'you mean?"

"It should be covered. There is a cover."

"It was covered with branches, unsecured at the ends, and a thin covering of earth and grass. Luckily one of the branches neither broke nor slipped, and Susan got her arm over it as she fell. Otherwise . . ."

Henry was staring into the hole.

"It goes down sheer for fifty feet," he said. "Then on in a rough tunnel, not so steep, for a quarter of a mile. It comes out at the entrance to our little creek, at low tide. At high, the last bit is under water."

"You *know* this place?"

"Of course. It has always been here." He turned to his companion and spoke to him in the Breton dialect. The man grunted and began to move in and out of the trees beside the clearing.

Susan stood away from Giles. She had stopped shivering, but she was still very pale. Her arm, the one that had taken her weight as she fell, was beginning to ache at the shoulder. She wondered if she had injured the joint, for when she tried to lift her hand to her hair, she found she could not do so. With an effort she said to Henry, "Is this the place where smugglers used to come up in the old days? And where they took kidnapped Germans down to the sea in the war? Francine tells ghastly stories about that."

"Yes. This is the place."

The man came back presently. Henry appeared to give him some detailed orders, for presently he lifted his beret in acknowledgement and went off towards the house. Henry shouldered the coil of rope.

"You have hurt your arm, Susan," he said. "Can you walk back?"

Giles pulled off the scarf he was wearing round his neck.

"Let me make you a sling," he offered. But Susan had turned away.

"Of course I can walk," she said, shortly, moving ahead of the two men. They fell in behind her, Giles last, and soon reached the house.

"I would prefer you not to tell Miriam what has happened," Henry said, in the hall.

"I wouldn't dream of it," Susan answered. "I have some sense."

"You'll have to account for that arm," said Giles. "Do let me fix it in a sling."

"I'll use one of my own scarves," said Susan, quietly, but with meaning. He understood, and admired her quick wits as much as he enjoyed their mild conspiracy.

"Thank you," Henry said, aware again of Susan's injury. "Is there anything . . . I mean, do you want anything . . ."

"Give the girl a good stiff drink!" Giles burst out, harshly, "and stop nattering about your wife."

He checked at once, furious with himself for having spoken in this way. "I beg your pardon," he said, stiffly, and moved off towards the stairs. Susan looked at him as he passed her. Her eyes were clouded and she did not speak. He went upstairs to find his friends.

Tony and Phillipa heard his story with some dismay and great astonishment.

"How could the cover get off the entrance hole?" Tony asked.

"Did Henry actually say it had a cover?"

"He did. And he certainly ordered the gardener chap or whatever he was, who came along with the rope, to look for something. He went about with his nose to the ground, obviously searching."

"Then it must have been taken off deliberately?"

"Quite deliberately."

"Why are you so sure?"

"I'll tell you. That seat was not in its proper place."

"Come again."

"The seat, the memorial seat, was in a postion where it did *not* command the view through the gap. I thought this was peculiar at the time. It ought to have been over the top of the hole."

"Can you be sure?"

"Quite sure. When I was clinging on to Susan, moving back slowly, and sticking my toes into the ground as I moved, I struck up against something solid, and hooked my instep round it. I had a look at it just before we left the clearing. It was a

short iron rod, fixed upright in the ground, with a screw thread
at the top. There was another on the other side of the hole. The
seat has rings at the side of the base. I don't mind betting they
fit over those rods with a nut to screw down over them. I'll have
a look tomorrow. But I expect the seat will be back over the
hole by then."

Phillipa was horrified.

"A deliberate trap?" she said, incredulous. "Someone laid a
trap for . . . someone?" she ended, lamely.

"Fun, isn't it?" Giles said. "There was a fifty foot drop, as
Henry so kindly told us."

"It *can't* have been meant for Susan," said Tony.

"I hope not. Or for me. No one knew we would use that
path. But Henry appeared very smartly at the precise moment
it was about to happen. I don't remember him calling out any
warning. But that could mean several things. Perhaps he was
there because he thought I was with Miriam. Perhaps he
thought she was with me, coming up the path. Susan was wearing her mackintosh."

"And hat?" asked Phillipa.

"No hat."

"Then he couldn't have mistaken her for his wife."

"The hair, you mean? All the same, the clearing is a favourite
spot of Miriam's."

"It doesn't look too good for Henry," agreed Tony.

CHAPTER VI

THE SUN SHONE the next day, though the wind still drove as hard as before. Thin white clouds raced across the blue overhead; above the horizon the sky was white with a yellow tinge.

"It will blow out today," Henry told his guests at breakfast time. "But the sea will not begin to go down until tomorrow. You must be patient for another day."

"We really can't impose on you any longer," Giles said. "It's been marvellous, sitting out the gale in comfort. But I do feel we ought to get back on board, and leave you in peace."

"In peace," repeated Henry, wrapping up the phrase in his accustomed gloom. The others, feeling embarrassed, looked down at their plates. Susan broke the silence with artificial gaiety.

"We ought to bathe," she proposed.

Phillipa shuddered.

"In this wind?"

"The creek is beautifully sheltered. The sun's hot enough."

"All right," said Giles, who welcomed any prolonged escape from the house. "We'll bathe. Good for my crew. They didn't take a stroke of exercise yesterday."

"We did." Tony was indignant. "We walked round the whole of Tréguier at least twice. And there's nothing more exhausting than trailing round a foreign town, trying to find the shops you want, which never seem to be where you'd expect them."

"A good swim is what you want," Giles insisted.

"You'll have to be careful not to go out too far," Henry warned them. "We usually bathe in the last hour of the flood. There's plenty of water then, with the mud and the rocks and the seaweed covered. It's perfectly safe at slack water, but don't stay in too long. It whistles out on the ebb and there are some nasty rocks at the entrance on our side."

"Where your tunnel comes out?" asked Giles.

58

Henry gave him a cold, hard stare, and nodded.

"But I thought you said the entrance rocks were covered when the tide was up?" Giles persisted.

"I was warning you of the ebb. The entrance *is* covered at high tide. But the outcrop of rock goes right out from the entrance of the tunnel to the beginning of the creek. There is a dangerous eddy round that corner when the water begins to go down."

"We'll remember," promised Tony.

The three friends went upstairs towards their rooms, taking Susan with them.

"I must write some letters," Phillipa said.

"You're always writing letters," Giles grumbled.

"That's all right," said Susan. "We can't bathe for hours. Anyway, I expect I'll have jobs to do for Miriam. I haven't seen her yet."

"According to Henry we ought not to go in before about one o'clock. High water is around two. But I should think we might go down at twelve."

"Will Henry be coming?" Tony asked.

"I shouldn't think so." Susan seemed doubtful. "He hardly ever does swim. And his back has been worse lately."

"What about Miriam?"

Phillipa's question was answered by gloomy looks from the men, but Susan laughed.

"Poor Miriam! But it's all right. She sunbathes a lot. I expect she'll come down in one of her lovely play suits and lie on the sand at her favourite spot. But she won't go in."

"Is there sand? I thought it was all mud."

"There's mostly a mixture. But there's a piece of sand not far from the rocks, just this side of the danger point."

They thought she was describing the same hazard that Henry had warned them of earlier, so they asked no more questions. Susan went away, and the Marshalls settled to writing postcards to their children. Giles wandered back downstairs and out into the garden. But the long grass was still wet from the storm, and the hot sun, sucking up the drops, was turning the whole enclosed space into a steam oven. He went back into the house, uneasy and restless, and filled with a great desire to leave the place. Something was going on there that he did not understand, and had no wish to take part in. Something dangerous; some evil, beginning to show itself, suddenly, startlingly, as in the averted accident to Susan the day before. No one spoke of it today. It might never have happened. It was not discussed, but it had not yet been explained. And there was a certainty, at least, of something planned, an organised wickedness. It had come to the surface in a seething moment of horror, and sunk back, leaving only a question, an uneasy dread. Giles was sure the lid would come off again, but when and where and how and against whom directed, he had no idea at all.

He went up to his room, intending to read for a while, but met Tony and Phillipa on the landing, about to take their mail to the post. He changed his mind, and went with them, taking his camera.

The village looked charming in the sun. As they reached the first cottages, they came to a stone trough of water, behind a low wall. Several women were kneeling round it, with baskets of laundry beside them. They flung the dirty clothes into the water, drew them out on to the stone slab round the trough, and scrubbed and pounded them there, before rinsing them again in the water. One old woman, in a wide white starched cap, looked up at them as they drew close. Giles stopped to take a photograph of her.

This caused a mild sensation. The other women looked up and laughed, and evidently teased the old lady. She got to her feet and came over to the wall.

"You have taken my photograph?" she asked, in a high quavering voice, with a strong Breton accent.

"Yes, madame. You don't mind?"

"With my capotte?"

She touched the crisp wings of her cap. Giles nodded.

"Tiens!" she said, and looked round at the younger women.

"I'll send you a copy," he promised, "if you give me your address."

This earned another round of applause and comment, but as no one made any move to give him the address, he began to walk away. He caught up Tony outside the grocer's shop, where the latter was standing, talking to Susan.

"Pip is buying coffee," Tony said. "She remembered we were running short on the boat. She said she was going to borrow the good lady's coffee mill to grind the beans."

"She could have used ours," said Susan.

"She likes chatting with the natives, or trying to, at least. Giles is our prize linguist."

Phillipa came out of the shop and they all walked back to the house.

"Henry is looked on with great respect," said Phillipa. "I felt rather grand when the grocer's wife said of course I could grind my coffee in her mill as I was a friend of the *seigneur* at the château."

"It only goes back to Henry's father, really," said Susan. "I believe he did a lot for Penguerrec between the wars, though they disapproved of him going to England when the second war started. He never came back, himself. Henry was over several times during the war, with the commandos, but he says the people here never quite forgave the old man for deserting them, as they called it."

Giles carried Susan's parcels. When they reached the house, he said to her, "I'm going down to open up *Shuna* and dry things out. Coming?"

"I'd love to. I'll just take the shopping to Francine."

She was back in a few minutes.

"Want any help?" asked Tony. But Phillipa drew him away.

"No. He doesn't. Don't forget to bring off the bathing things, Giles," she reminded him, as the two went out into the sunlight.

"I'll see he doesn't," Susan called back, happily.

The river was flowing quietly again, and *Shuna* sat peacefully on its waters, her white topsides, washed by the rain, gleaming in the sun.

"Isn't she lovely!" Susan exclaimed, as they came out on to the landing-stage.

"She is that, and more," Giles answered.

When they went aboard they found the rain had made one or two damp patches in the cabin, but on the whole the bunks and bedding did not seem wet. While Susan took the sleeping-bags and blankets on deck, to hang them over the boom in the sun, Giles went over the rigging and ropes, to check any damage the gale might have caused. He found nothing to worry him unduly, and nothing he could not put right, except for a block caught under a halliard at the top of the mast.

"I'll have to wait for that till I get Tony back on board," he told Susan.

"Why?"

"Because you can't hoist me in the bosun's chair, I'm too heavy, and I can't hoist you, because you don't know what to do when you get there."

"Can't you tell me?"

He smiled at her.

"Want to go aloft? It's quite a way. Sure you won't get giddy looking down?"

"After looking down that hole in the ground yesterday, hanging by one arm, I should think this will be a picnic."

He felt sudden concern.

"Your arm? I haven't even asked after it today."

She laughed.

"It's quite recovered. You'd all have known about it if it hadn't been."

"All right. You only have to unsnarl that block that won't shake free."

He got out the bosun's chair, fixed it to the main halliard, told Susan how to sit in it, and how to steady herself against the mast, and began to haul her up. There was a hitch at the first cross-trees, which she negotiated clumsily. But with a few more shouted instructions from Giles, she slipped past the second cross-trees without difficulty, and reached the captive block. She freed it without much difficulty.

"What's it like up there?" Giles called to her.

"Fine. I can just see the chimneys of the house."

"Want to stay up?"

"Not particularly."

"Hold on, then. I'll bring you down."

She let herself slip out of the chair as it came near the deck, and landed neatly on her feet beside him. She was near, very near, her eyes and hair were shining, her cheeks flushed from excitement and the sun. Giles caught her to him, and with their first long kiss felt the sad remains of his regard for Miriam dissolve from his heart for ever.

"What about the bathe?" said Susan, presently.

She was astonished and dizzy with happiness, but she remembered Miriam, and did not know yet that her cousin's wife no longer held any power over Giles.

"Yes." He was quite glad to come back to earth. Rocket flight had its disadvantages. "You go below and rummage out the bathing suits and towels. I think you'll find them in the lockers at the for'ard end of the cabin. Mine are in a drawer under my bunk, aft. The quarter-berth on the port side."

She went below, and Giles, having stowed the bosun's chair again, and made up the halliard, went forward to the anchor chain.

"What are you doing now?" Susan asked, putting her head up through the forehatch.

"Letting down some more chain."

"I heard it rattling. I thought you were weighing anchor. Isn't that what you say? I wondered where we were going."

He grinned at her.

"Hardly likely to cast loose, without a sail up or the engine on."

"I suppose not. Why more chain?"

"Because it's coming up to springs. High tides, ten feet at least higher than neaps. That means that at the top of the flood she'll ride ten feet higher from the bottom of the river."

"I see. Why do the tides do all that? Change, I mean?"

"The moon. You get spring tides with the new moon and the full, and neaps at the half."

"Every fortnight, then?"

"That's the idea."

Giles made the anchor chain fast. He and Susan put away the

aired bedding below. Then they rowed back to the stage.

They found that the Marshalls had already started for the creek. Francine came into the hall to give them this message.

"Monsieur Henri is working, and begs to be excused," she went on.

"On a lovely day like this?" Giles exclaimed. "After being cooped up for two days."

"He took a walk before he went to the library, monsieur."

"And Madame?" Susan asked.

"Madame is sunbathing, as usual."

"That'll be at the creek," the girl explained to Giles. "I told you, she has a favourite spot on the sand. Tony and Pip will find her there."

But this had not happened. As Giles and Susan came to the outer fringe of the trees above the creek, they met Miriam on her way back.

"I've given up," she said, in an exhausted voice. "I got as far as this, but my head is quite awful. I'm going back to lie down."

Susan cried sympathetically, "You poor thing!" But Giles said, "Did you see the others?"

"They've gone on. They are rather annoyed with you for taking so long over fetching the bathing things. They have Henry's shrimp nets. They are going shrimping until you arrive."

Susan gave her a worried look.

"Shall I come back with you?"

"By no means. Giles would be very angry with me."

There was a concentrated venom in her voice that made them both recoil and flooded Susan's cheeks with scarlet.

Giles looked stonily at Miriam. She was wearing a big floppy sun hat, and a strapless, skirtless, play suit in gay flowered cotton. Her body was tanned an attractive brown, Giles thought, and her face was as lovely as ever. But he rejoiced to find that his immunity held firmly in her presence. He even felt detached enough to pity her.

"I expect it's the sudden swing back in the weather," he said. "Your headache, I mean."

"Perhaps," she answered, quietly enough. "But it is also the things that have happened." She turned suddenly to Susan and cried passionately, "You should have told me!"

"Told you?"

"That the ground gave way. That you might have been killed!"

Giles said gravely, "How did you find out? Henry asked us not to say anything. He wasn't going to tell you. He thought you'd be too much upset."

"Isn't it worse not to be told?" Miriam's voice was hoarse with terrified self-pity. "Besides, it is not the sort of thing that can be kept secret. Louis knew, because he helped Henry to fetch the rope, so of course he told the maids, and they told Francine, and she told me."

She broke off, shutting her eyes and screwing up her face in pain.

"Let me take you back to the house," urged Susan.

"No! No! You want to bathe. Go and bathe. I won't be a nuisance to anyone. I am used to suffering alone."

She staggered away with a tragic gait, but they noticed as they watched her, that very soon she changed this for a normal walk, and quite a brisk one at that.

"Poor thing," sighed Susan. "If only she wouldn't build everything up, so."

Giles said nothing. They went down to the creek in silence.

The tide was coming in fast, but it had not yet reached the strip of sand near the rocks at the seaward end of the creek. Some whitewashed cottages on the other side of the water were reflected in its smooth blue surface. A few gulls wheeled overhead.

"It looks so peaceful in here," said Susan.

"And in the river," Giles agreed. "The wind is taking off all the time. With luck the sea will be down enough to get away tomorrow."

"In the afternoon?"

"It would have to be. Yes. Or perhaps the next morning, early."

"You aren't so keen to dash away as you were at first."

E

He put out a hand to draw her to him.

"You know who's responsible for that."

He saw her answering smile change to a look of bewilderment.

"What's wrong?"

She swung round, pointing.

"The notice. Henry's 'Danger' notice. It's gone!"

"No. It hasn't. I can see it. Tony and Pip were hiding it before they moved on."

He was pulling her back, but she tore herself away and started to run. He heard her shouting, "Come back, both of you! Come back!"

Not understanding anything but the urgency of her action, he followed. He saw his friends stop, stand still, with their shrimping nets resting on the sand, wave and begin to turn. And then to his horror he saw Tony flounder, heard his yell of astonishment and fear, and saw that he was already up to his knees in the sand. Immediately he understood Susan's action.

"Lie down!" he shouted, as he began to run. "Lie down on the shrimp nets!"

Phillipa, who seemed to be on firm sand, pushed her net back towards her husband. He flung himself forward on to his own, and wriggling desperately, managed to catch hold of hers. By this time Susan had reached them. She and Phillipa, gripping the handle of the net, tugged at it with all their strength. But it was not until Giles reached them, adding his weight to theirs, that Tony began to move. Once his knees were free, his legs came out more easily, and they were able to shuffle back quickly. But Giles would not stop or let Tony get up until they were above tide level.

"We went by the notice," said Tony, indignantly, when he was once more on his feet, and they had all got back their breath.

Susan nodded. Her face was very white.

"The notice has been moved," she said.

"*Moved?*"

"It ought to be back there, in line with that fallen tree trunk and the sticking-out rock at the edge of the sand. The other side of that line is safe. This side is not. I mean, below the water-line."

"Quicksand," said Pip. She was still trembling with shock. "Henry said something about no one being able to get to the tunnel's mouth by land. Only by sea."

Giles nodded. "So that was what he meant."

"Yes."

"It hasn't been moved far," Susan pointed out. "I shouldn't have noticed it, I think, if you two hadn't moved in front of it when I was looking at you. Then I saw it was the wrong side of the rock."

"If you feel all right," Giles said quietly to Tony, "I suggest we get back to the safe side of the line and have our bathe."

"I'm all for it," he answered. "That was mud under the sand, and stinking mud at that. I'd like to wash it off."

They enjoyed their bathe, though none of them went out very far, nor did they attempt to put their feet down once they had taken to the water, though Susan assured them that the beach shelved steeply and they were safely out of their depth almost at once, and well above the treacherous mud.

As they were walking up through the wood afterwards, Giles went ahead with Tony.

"Did you happen to see Miriam on the beach?" he asked him.

"Yes. She was down there when we arrived."

"Sunbathing?"

"No. Standing at the edge of the trees. She waved, and we went up to speak to her. She was all dressed up for the beach, but she didn't stay."

"No. We met her, too. She had a raging headache, she said, and was going back to the house."

"I see."

As they walked up the last sweep of the drive, they saw Henry, sitting in a deck chair in the sun.

"The work must have gone sour on him," said Giles.

"Or he may have finished his stint for the day."

They went up to him.

"Enjoyed your bathe?" asked Henry.

They began to tell him what had happened. Before they had

finished, Susan and Phillipa came up and Miriam appeared from the house. She had put on a skirt that matched her beach suit, and also a bolero, with short sleeves. Giles finished his account of the mishap.

Henry was suitably upset.

"Some stupid louts from the village, I expect," he said, angrily. "Probably playing around and knocked over the notice and stuck it up again without bothering to look where they put it."

"I suppose they'd think it was quite potty to need a notice at all," suggested Phillipa. "They must all know from childhood exactly where the quicksands are likely to be."

"Henry has known it from childhood," said Miriam, softly.

There was an awkward pause. Then Tony said, looking at her sternly, "Your headache must have prevented *you* from noticing the sign had been moved."

"Oh, I never go anywhere near it," she answered, easily.

"That's a lie," whispered Susan, under her breath.

"Headache?" asked Henry. His face showed real concern.

"We seem to have been the only people to enjoy your beach," said Phillipa.

"A mixed enjoyment," Susan added.

"Oh, I was down there before any of you," said Henry, lightly. "I always have a walk before breakfast. Actually, it was the other side of the creek I visited today. The village side of it."

"So you wouldn't see your notice at that distance? Or would you?"

"Unfortunately I didn't, did I?" said Henry.

Again there was silence. Then they all went indoors.

CHAPTER VII

IT NOW SEEMED clear to the party from *Shuna* that they must get away from the château as soon as they could. The atmosphere in the house had become unbearable, weighed down as it was with suspicion and terror. No one was taking any steps to clear up the growing mystery. Instead Henry retreated more and more from public view and Miriam was working herself into an even wilder state of emotional tension than ever before.

The second near-accident, the second trap, as she loudly proclaimed it, was directed at her, and at her alone. She reached this conclusion half-way through luncheon, announcing it with the maximum of dramatic effect, to the great embarrassment of her hearers.

Suddenly putting down her knife and fork she said, in a low tense voice, "I have escaped twice, haven't I? I can't expect to escape a third time. How do I know I am not being poisoned at this very minute?"

Henry gave a short, unpleasant laugh.

"If you are, so are the rest of us."

Phillipa made an effort to check the ridiculous scene.

"I don't know why you think the traps, as you call them, were meant for you. They seem to me to have been laid pretty indiscriminately. Probably by village louts, as Henry suggests. Anyone might have fallen into either of them."

Giles took this up.

"Exactly," he said. "As it happened, Susan sprang the first, and Tony the second."

Miriam got up slowly, pushing her plate away.

"I feel ill," she said, faintly. "I think I am poisoned."

In spite of themselves, the others watched her with feelings of chill alarm. Her excessive fear swept from her to them all blotting out reason and even common sense. She looked ill; she must be ill for her face to take on that greyish tinge. Her dark eyes, fixed on Henry, at the head of the table, were wild with despair and a vision of death. She seemed to be disintegrating before their eyes.

Giles and Tony started up: Susan was already on her feet. They reached her as she fell, and caught her, and the two men carried her to her room.

Left alone with Henry, who had not moved from his seat, Phillipa said, in a shocked voice, "Aren't you even going to call a doctor?"

That roused him. He got up with a violent movement, nearly knocking over his chair.

"Yes, I will do the correct thing," he said, harshly. "I will call the doctor, and when he comes the hysterical fit will be over, as usual, and he will be told it was my fault, as usual. She turns this house into a bedlam, but it is my fault! Always my fault! I am responsible. *I* have created the fantasy in which she lives."

He brought his fist down on the table, making the dishes rattle.

"This is not all imagined," said Phillipa, steadily. "The uncovered hole was real, and the moved warning post. They were real, and dangerous; deadly dangerous. How do you really explain those things? I should like to know what you are doing to find the answers? And the culprits? My husband was very nearly caught by the sand, you know."

His eyes went blank. He picked up his dinner napkin to wipe his mouth.

"Our village boys," he muttered. "Primitive. Peasant minds, still."

His gaze went aimlessly round the room.

"I'm very sorry," he mumbled on. "Very unfortunate. Not used to visitors. My wife, I mean. Make her worse. And Giles turning up. So extraordinary. I apologise. Will you excuse me. The doctor . . ."

He went out of the room, leaving Phillipa, astonished, alone at the table.

"They're both crackers," she announced a little later.

Giles and Tony had joined her in the Marshalls' bedroom. They nodded gloomily.

"I think we ought to leave here at once," she went on.

"So do I," Tony agreed. "I'd feel a darned sight safer with the sea under me than the less than solid earth of this peculiar spot. Makes you wonder what'll give way next."

"Frankly, I'd have gone already, if it hadn't been for Susan," said Giles, boldly.

"She's only staying the summer, isn't she?"

"I know, Pip. She's only got another month here. Thank God, she won't be able to stay longer than that, because her parents will be arriving home and she has to get the house open for them."

"You'll be able to get in touch then, won't you?"

"That's not the point," Giles turned away from them. "I'd like to get her out of this, now. I don't understand what goes on here. I don't like it. Why don't they have a doctor for Miriam?"

"Henry said he would call her doctor. That was before he went all peculiar, himself."

"She needs a doctor and a proper nurse. Then Susan would be free to leave. It isn't as if they needed help in the house. This isn't England. Francine has plenty of domestic help, and she runs that side damned efficiently."

Phillipa understood what he was trying to say.

"You want to stay until the doctor has been? Is that it? And try to persuade Susan to leave?"

He nodded.

"I'd like to take her with us."

"On *Shuna*, old boy?" asked Tony, in surprise.

"Why not? For a few days, to let things simmer down here. Or come to a head, whichever happens. We've lost four days, but we still have time, if the weather picks up, to see a bit more of this coast before we start back."

"We've no objection, have we, Tony?" Phillipa urged.

"On the contrary."

"Then I suggest we take our gear back to the boat this afternoon, and go off on the morning tide. That'll give us time to keep an eye on developments here, and get Susan to make up her mind."

He went to his room, determined to put his plan into action

at once. It did not take long to pack the few clothes he had
brought ashore. But when his bag was filled, he went across to
the window, to stand there, staring out at the imprisoning
trees.

He heard the door of the room open. Thinking it was Tony
come to tell him he was ready to go down to the boat, he did
not move, only said, "If I owned this place, the first thing I'd
do would be to clear a proper space round the house."

He heard Francine's voice behind him say, "Monsieur!"
and swung round to face her.

"If you please, Monsieur, Madame wishes to speak to you."

"But she's ill," he cried, exasperated by this demand.
"Hasn't the doctor been? Oughtn't she to be kept very quiet?"

"Monsieur Henri telephoned to the doctor, and he will
come. But Madame says she will not see him, because she is not
ill."

"That's ridiculous! She must see him. I think she is very
ill."

"She is not ill, monsieur. It is not illness. It is despair."

He was outraged. He snapped out, "Nonsense!" and picking
up his bag, made for the door. As he reached it, Francine stood
aside. There was a baffled look in her eyes, and she was breathing heavily.

"I implore you, monsieur," she said, and her restraint and
evident sincerity moved him. He paused, looking intently at
her.

"Are you sure this is not just another bout of hysteria?" he
asked. He used that all-embracing term *"Crise des nerfs"*,
which can cover anything from a fit of temper to a mental
breakdown.

"I swear it is not," she answered. "On the contrary, it is the
last appeal of a breaking heart."

The extravagance of this statement restored all of Giles's
former hostility. But he felt committed.

"Very well," he said. "I will speak to her. I had intended to
send her a message to say goodbye and thank you. But I will see
her for a few minutes instead."

"Thank you, monsieur," said Francine, "and God bless

you." She added, in a low voice, so that he only just heard, "Be kind to her, monsieur. She loves you."

Giles strode away, these outrageous words ringing in his ears, stirring up memories that he knew no longer had power to move him, but which he still feared.

He came to Miriam's room, knocked, and went in.

She was not in bed, but was lying on a sofa drawn up near the window. She had taken off her beach clothes and was wearing a dressing-gown of transparent nylon and lace, through which he saw clearly her brown skin and scanty under-clothes.

"You have come!" she said, in her most theatrical manner. "Thank God!"

He was sickened by the whole stupid, seedy business, the false emptiness of the situation, his own unwilling participation.

"Look here, Miriam," he said. "You've got to understand things as they really are. For heaven's sake stop this sordid play-acting. There is no point in it, and you are making your-self ill."

Her eyes filled with tears. She turned her head away.

"If *you* don't believe me, then there is no hope," she said. "No possible chance to escape. I am doomed."

In spite of the extravagant language, in spite of his conviction that her fears were groundless, he felt a pang of dread catch at his own heart. After all, strange things *had* happened. Things for which he had no explanation. And Henry was an odd character. A bit sinister, if you liked to see him that way.

"But I don't see *why!*" he cried, answering his own unspoken question.

Miriam turned. The tears were dried; instead her eyes shone with a feverish brightness.

"You don't believe what I told you, Giles, do you? You think it is unbelievable that Henry would want to get rid of me? You are wrong. He is very plausible. He pretends to be so respectable, so dull. But he has a secret life. Why else should he go away so often, without explanation, without leaving an address?"

"Does he do that?"

"He does. He simply tells me he is going away. For a fortnight. For three weeks. It varies. He says he is going, but I never know if he will come back."

"But he does come back?"

"So far he has come back."

"I don't see that that sort of behaviour can be made to prove he wants to get rid of you—by violence. It would tend to suggest he might some day simply walk out on you."

She looked at him so sorrowfully that he was ashamed of what he had said.

"You are very hard, Giles. You have never forgiven me."

"Rubbish!"

"I was wrong to break our engagement, Giles. I have so often repented it, since. But I was afraid of being poor, and you had very little money then, hadn't you? Not like now."

The poor fool, he thought, does she really think this is the sort of talk to move me?

"Henry was so romantic at that time, Giles. The thought of the château, the people all devoted to him. And he took me about to such lovely places, where I had never been with you."

She saw his face harden, and his eyes grow flinty. She could not understand what she had done. She had quite forgotten the intermediate George, who made a nonsense of these wistful explanations.

"I really came in to see you to say goodbye and thank you for having us here," Giles said, awkwardly, afraid of a fresh outburst of tears or protests.

But Miriam indulged in neither. She put out a hand and laid it simply in his. He let his fingers close on it, suddenly wrung by pity for her.

"Will you kiss me goodbye, Giles?" she asked. "I was going to ask you to take me with you, but I see that it would be no good. You would refuse."

He leaned over her, and touched her cheek, feeling nothing. Susan, he rejoiced in his heart, Susan darling, I'm free of her at last.

"Why don't you go to England for a bit and see some of your old friends?" he said, stroking her hair, and speaking to her as if she were a child.

"I have no friends," she answered.

He straightened up and she took her hand away. She seemed to have retreated into some far corner of her being.

"I should like to say goodbye to the others," she said, with cold dignity.

"You're not well. I'll say it for you."

"I'm perfectly well. I'll join you in the hall in five minutes."

He could do nothing to prevent this, so he went away to find the Marshalls and tell them what Miriam intended.

They looked for Henry downstairs, but were told he had gone down to the creek to attend to the warning notice.

While they were waiting for Miriam, Susan came into the hall. Giles drew her to one side.

"We are taking our gear back on board," he said, "and going off tomorrow, early. I must see you before then."

"Does Miriam know?"

"She knows. She is coming down to the stage with us now."

"But . . ."

"I know. Darling, I must see you."

She looked troubled. He caught her hand and held it.

"Henry will think it very odd if you go off without any warning," she said. "It will look as if this morning's mishap on the beach has scared you all away."

He laughed.

"As far as the Marshalls are concerned, he'd be dead right. But I see your point."

"Come back to tea. Or at least for drinks, later. He's almost certain to make you stop for dinner."

"Wouldn't he think we were scrounging a last meal off him?"

"Of course not. Oh, look, here she is!"

Susan snatched her hand away, with an uneasy feeling that Miriam had watched the movement, and understood its full implications.

"So sorry to have kept you all waiting," the latter said, sweetly. "Shall we start?"

Nobody talked much on the way down through the wood. The two men strode ahead, carrying the bags, and the three women, in single file, Miriam leading, came after. Consequently the second group was soon left far behind, while Giles and Tony disappeared from their view.

Phillipa would have preferred to go faster. She and Susan were carrying the oilskins of the yachting party. While not as heavy as the bags, they were heavy enough, and their smell, combined with the heat, and the many flies that attacked the party as they moved, made the walk extremely disagreeable. But Miriam did not seem to notice the discomfort of her companions. She fanned herself with a bunch of leaves as she went along, planting her feet very carefully to avoid brambles.

When at last they arrived near the edge of the wood, Phillipa put down her burden to cool her arms.

"Oilskins are the last word on a hot day," she exclaimed.

"Hear, hear!" agreed Susan.

"I'm absolutely dripping. I feel ready for another bathe."

"So do I."

Miriam went on, paying no attention, and presently the others gathered up the oilskins again and followed her.

When the stage came into view Susan stopped again.

"Henry!" she exclaimed. "He's talking to Giles. I thought . . ."

"We were *told*," said Phillipa, with cold emphasis, "that he had gone to the creek."

"I suppose he could have gone there first, and come on here."

"Without passing us?"

"Oh, yes. There are plenty of paths through the wood."

"So it seems."

They moved on again. Miriam was some distance from them now. She had not altered her pace on seeing Henry. She simply continued as before, fanning herself as she went.

"I don't see Tony," Susan said.

"He'll be getting the dinghy ready. Putting the bags into it. We can't see the third part of the stage from here. It's down the ladder a bit by now."

"Yes, of course."

They came up with the group on the bank.

"Were you told we were coming down?" she asked Henry, cheerfully. "Or was it intuition?"

"I was told," he answered, quite seriously. "I took a short cut."

"As you and Miriam are both here," said Giles, "why not come off and have a look round *Shuna?*

It was said from politeness only. He did not imagine either of them would accept. But Miriam greeted the idea with exaggerated pleasure.

"Yes, we will," she said. "How do we get there? In that tiny little coracle?"

"It holds four."

"But there are six of us."

"The cannibals and the missionaries," laughed Henry, unexpectedly. "How will you do it?"

"Tony can take the bags off, with Pip and Susan, and come back for the rest of us."

"Susan has been on board before," protested Miriam. "I'll go with Pip and the luggage."

She clambered agilely on to the first ladder, showing none of the nervous ineptitude that Phillipa, for one, expected. There was a crack, a splintering sound, and the ladder swivelled outwards and then fell back against the staging with a loud clang.

Miriam screamed. Tony, below, stooping over the dinghy, was nearly pitched forward into it, as the second stage swung out and back, pulling the third stage with it.

"Hi!" he shouted. "What the devil . . . !"

He swung round and saw Giles seize Miriam's shoulder in a strong grip and pull her back off the ladder. He ran to the foot of it.

"Don't come up," said Henry, from above. He was kneeling on the staging, leaning over its edge. "The tie up here has pulled out."

"You're telling me! Can't you hold the darned thing? I'll put my weight on that side to hold it in."

The tide had not gone down very far yet. Tony had only

about six feet of ladder to negotiate. He stepped up gingerly and after two rungs was able to get his arms on to the stage and pull himself up to it without using the ladder.

"Well, well!" he said, as he stood upright. "Your property seems to be giving way in all directions, doesn't it?"

Henry looked up at him, but said nothing, only let go the top of the ladder and got to his feet, brushing his knees.

The group on the bank was strangely, ominously quiet. Miriam's behaviour, as usual, dominated and directed the response of them all. And Miriam, after that one terrified scream, stood silent and rigid, with her tragic eyes fixed on her husband. It was not difficult to interpret that gaze.

Giles was suddenly furious

"Why the devil don't you say something!" he shouted at Henry. "Why don't you *do* something about these fantastic accidents? This one, at least, was normal wear and tear."

He knelt, brushing away the dust from the splintered wood, exposing the rusted broken bolt that had caused the mishap.

"Might have happened any time in the last year or so, I should think," he said, more quietly.

Miriam spoke, in a high, unnatural voice.

"Without you, Giles, I should have fallen, as I was meant to fall."

"Oh, rubbish, Miriam," cried Phillipa, outraged by this preposterous statement. "You don't mean that. You can't mean it!"

"You wouldn't have fallen far," said Giles, roughly. "If at all. More than half the ladder is under water. The second bit of staging would hold it in, stop it falling right outwards, even if both sides of the top came off, instead of only one."

She paid no attention at all to this.

"I was meant to fall," she repeated.

Henry at last roused himself from the apparent stupor into which he had fallen. He stepped forward and took his wife by the arm.

"Come," he said. "You are not well. I will take you back to the house."

They all expected another outburst of hysteria, another

scene. But this did not happen. Instead Miriam gave in. Her
head drooped, her body seemed to shrink and age. She did not
attempt to shake off Henry's restraining hand, but let him lead
her away into the trees. And at that moment her own convinced premonition of death so affected all the watchers that
they moved involuntarily a few steps after her, driven by an
impulse to snatch her back from that unavoidable doom.

CHAPTER VIII

IT WAS PHILLIPA who stopped them.

"Let's go on board," she said. "We can do no good here."

Tony turned towards the landing-stage.

"Hold the ladder in, Giles, while I go down again," he said.

But Giles was looking at Susan.

"Is that true?" he asked, in a troubled voice. "Is there nothing we can do?"

"Why ask me?" she said. "Why not ask Miriam?"

"You don't mean that," he answered, going to help Tony.

She did not, but she was so confused by the most recent event that she now felt nothing but resentment. Only not against Giles, she reminded herself, ashamed of her own churlishness.

She went forward and stood beside him. He was still holding the ladder, for Phillipa this time. When she was safely on the stage below, he handed the bags down to Tony.

"I'm sorry I said that," Susan told him. "I'm a bit rattled by what's happening."

He looked up at her and grinned, then scrambled to his feet.

"You've every right to be. If we only knew what *is* happening."

"Do you think Miriam is mad?"

He looked at her.

"Do you?"

"No."

"Neither do I. But I'm damned if I know whether she's play-acting deliberately for some obscure reason, or if she can't help herself."

"If she can't help it, then it means she's genuinely frightened."

"Of Henry? Can you believe that?"

She shook her head.

"No, I can't. In his own way he's fond of her. I know he is.

And he's worried to death about her—as well as about himself."

"I know."

"His back has been worse this last week. And something else is wrong. Haven't you noticed how swollen his hands are?"

"Can't say I have. But I haven't looked particularly. He got down on his knees quite briskly to look at the ladder. But that could have been in the excitement of the moment. He went off walking rather slowly."

"His ankles were swollen this morning, too, Francine told me."

Tony and Phillipa were sitting in the dinghy, waiting. They had the luggage piled in the bows of the little boat.

"Shall we take this off, and come back for you two?" Tony called.

"You do that. Bring a bit of rope back, so I can fix this ladder for the last one down."

Tony pushed off. Giles and Susan sat on the bank to wait.

"This last scare was a genuine accident," said Giles, after a time. "The wood is rotten and it gave way. It might have gone any time. No one could possibly arrange for it to go the precise moment Miriam got on to the ladder. Besides, Tony had already used it."

"I know. It was sheer bad luck it had to be Miriam."

"And it was sheer bad luck for some criminal or other it had to be you who was caught in the first trap, and Tony in the second."

"They *were* traps, then, were they?"

"They damned well were. Pretty sinister ones, too. And noticeably of the same pattern."

"How do you mean?"

"In each case there would have been a disappearance, without obvious cause, and *without trace.*"

Susan drew a long breath.

"Of course. The seat would have been put back over the cover, which would have been put back over the hole. And the notice would have been put back in its real place."

"Exactly. But the main question is this. Who were those

F

traps set to catch? I know that Miriam used to go and sit on the memorial seat to enjoy the view in solitude. And she used to sunbathe on the sand near the warning notice. But surely if she made a habit of going to these places, you'd expect her to know them so well she'd notice any change in them, immediately. She may be neurotic, but she's no fool."

"Yes. I'm sure you're right. If the traps were meant for Miriam, they were very clumsily thought out. But suppose they were not meant for her?"

"Who then?"

"Me, perhaps. Or even you."

"In heaven's name, *why?*"

She looked at him, steadily.

"We are assuming all the time that Henry has done these things, aren't we?"

"I suppose so. Who else could it be?"

"I'm wondering about Francine."

"Francine!"

"Yes."

"But she seems to be devoted to Miriam. Actually she's tackled both Pip and myself on the subject."

He laughed self-consciously, and Susan pretended to be indignant.

"On the strength of your old attachment, I suppose? Does she think it still operates? In any case, how did she find out about it?"

"Snooping, I gather from Pip. She might take a sentimental view, I suppose. But she's French. I don't think it's likely. Just wishful thinking, perhaps."

"I was a bit doubtful about you, myself, at first. But not for long."

He gave her a quick kiss, and another, more prolonged.

"She practically accused me of making Miriam unhappy, so I suppose she may really have noticed you and me getting to like each other, and wanted to get rid of me. A bit drastic, though."

"Impossible, really. I'm being fanciful. She knows you are going as soon as you can. You've been trying to get away ever since you came. Besides, respectable French housekeepers don't go in for crime."

"With a few notable exceptions. However, I think we can cut out Francine, however much she sympathises with Miriam. Besides, she wouldn't be capable of doing the actual physical work of preparing those traps. I mean, moving the seat, and the notice board."

"No, of course not. Silly of me. Wash that out."

"So it must be Henry. But you may be right about the intended victim. It is quite on the cards that Henry might want to get rid of *me*. Miriam described him as a sort of obscure ogre, but I didn't believe a word of it at the time."

"He isn't. He is never very forthcoming, but then he is never really well. I can't say I know him at all, though. And I've been here nearly two months."

"I thought he behaved in a rather sinister manner just now. He did nothing whatever to help Miriam, or to comfort her afterwards. Simply took her off with him as if she'd been a dog in disgrace."

Susan shivered, and drew closer to Giles. He put an arm round her.

"Why don't you come with us? For a day or two, at least. While we're cruising on this side."

She said, wistfully, "If only I could."

"Then why not . . .?"

"Look," she said, scrambling to her feet, "here's Tony back with the dinghy."

By this time the wind had dropped to a light breeze. The sun shone brilliantly from a clear sky. The open channel in the distance beyond the mouth of the river, looked very inviting.

"I wish we were going *now*," said Phillipa.

They were all four sitting about the deck, while Phillipa dispensed tea from the cockpit.

"Better tomorrow morning," Giles corrected. "If we're going on east to Lézardrieux we need to take the latter part of the ebb out of here, so that by the time we're clear of the rocks at Les Heaux it'll have turned and be in our favour again along

the coast and into the next river. I haven't done my sums yet,
but that's the general idea."

"We'll be starting between five and six tomorrow morning,
then?" Tony asked.

"Something like that. Unless you want to try the inside
channel, the mainland side of Les Heaux."

"No, we don't," said Phillipa, emphatically. "We want to
avoid all possible hazards from now on."

"You can't do it on this coast," Giles reminded her.

After tea he took Susan for a row in the dinghy. They
drifted down the river on the tide without much effort, and
landed on the other side of the water, at the hard below Pen
Paluch. They pulled the dinghy up the beach, fastened the
painter to a ring in the little harbour wall, and walked up the
hill.

The village here lay more steeply than Penguerrec. The
houses were terraced and the narrow road climbed up and
round and back again. There seemed to be only one shop in the
place, but they had not come to buy stores, only to explore and
be together.

They walked on through the village and found a country
road. It had a good surface and tall hedges. Too tall, Giles
complained, to see where they were. When they came to a gate,
he climbed it and stood precariously on top, balancing himself
with the help of a small tree in the hedge.

"Plougrescant church is dead ahead," he reported. "We
might go and look at it."

Susan laughed.

"It's about six miles from here by road," she said. "You
can't go direct anywhere. All fields and winding lanes. Just like
Devon."

"Right. Then we'll find a nice secluded field and enjoy the
sun."

There were flies in the field, and the sun was very hot, far
hotter than on the boat in the river. But Susan and Giles were
much too engrossed with one another to notice these discom-
forts. Later, when the sun had left their corner of the field,
sinking down now to the west, they went back to the harbour

hand in hand, and rowed slowly up to *Shuna*, unhindered by the tide, which was nearly at slack water.

Susan wanted to go straight back to the house, because she had been away so long, but the others persuaded her to have dinner on board. Afterwards Giles took her to the landing-stage and walked with her up the path through the woods.

At the edge of the lawn he stopped.

"I won't come to the house," he said. "I've written this final note to Miriam, simply thanking her from the three of us for her hospitality. Will you give it to her, and a similar message to Henry?"

She promised to do this.

"Write to me at Peter Port," Giles said. "We ought to be there in three or four days from now. And take care of yourself."

He kissed her and went away, and Susan watched him until he was out of sight. Then she went into the house.

They turned in early on *Shuna*, because they had to be up at dawn the next day. Giles lay awake for a long time, listening to the quiet breathing of his sleeping crew, and the gentle slapping of the river against the sides of the yacht. Susan was his girl, he decided, and he meant to marry her. This affair was not make-believe, like all the other encounters with which he had tried to solace himself since Miriam broke out of his life so cruelly. And so disastrously, it seemed, to her own happiness. He lay awake, knowing that he would marry Susan, and wondering what his life would have been like if he had married Miriam. She and Henry had no children. Perhaps that was partly the cause of her present pitiable state. But it might be her own fault, not her misfortune, and not Henry's selfishness. In that case he could be thankful she had let him down. And again his thoughts went round to her strange insistence upon danger and death, her obsession with fear, her wild attempts to renew her power over him. Without Susan's presence and all that it had come to mean for him in these few days, he knew he would have been lost. Even now, he realised with dismay, he was thinking more of Miriam than of his new young love. At last he fell asleep, adding his own quiet breathing to that of his sleeping friends.

The tide came in, filling the creek, rising up the river banks. The landing-stage rode level under the full moon. Not a breath of wind stirred the rigging. And at the turn of the tide, about three in the morning, *Shuna* began to move. Her bows swung gently round, as they always did, to face upstream to meet the current beginning to flow towards the sea. But she did not only turn, she began almost at once to slide down the river. Faster and faster she moved, swinging sideways now, borne along by the rush of the ebb, towards the sea and the jagged rocks round which the eddies surged and swept.

A fishing boat had come into the river that night, bound for Tréguier. She did not belong to either of the villages at the mouth of the river, and had no moorings of her own in their harbours. She had not picked up any of the empty moorings, but had dropped her anchor in the stream just clear of the other boats, trusting to the late hour to save her from any trouble with other shipping.

Shuna was swept broadside on into the bows of this vessel, with a crash that woke everyone on board.

Giles was on deck in a matter of seconds. At first he thought the fishing boat had run into him, in spite of the full moon and the riding light he always hung from his forestay. But he realised almost at once that the fishing boat was fast at her anchor and *Shuna* was the truant.

The crew of the fishing vessel had gone ashore to spend the night with friends. There was no one aboard. Giles and Tony made *Shuna* fast to her, and as the first grey light began to drown the shadows of the moon, they inspected the damage. A considerable amount of paint had gone, the gunwale was badly dented in several places. Two of the stanchions to which the life-lines were fastened had carried away, but otherwise, above the waterline *Shuna* had come off fairly well.

"We were lucky to hit a boat," said Tony, "and not a fixed target like a rock."

"A rock would probably have holed us," answered Giles.

He looked dazed and bewildered.

"I can't think how it happened," he kept repeating. "We

held in the gale, so why not tonight, with no wind at all?"

"Springs," said Tony. "We must have pulled up our anchor."

"But I let down an extra five fathoms this morning—I mean yesterday morning—on purpose," said Giles. "Give me the torch!" he added, quickly.

Going forward he stooped over the chain, and swore fiercely.

"Come here, Tony!" he shouted.

Tony went quickly up to the bows.

"Look at the figures on the chain," Giles said. "Lucky I painted them all on fresh this season. The fathoms are in red."

"Someone has taken in the chain."

"Someone who knew exactly how far to take it in to guarantee we'd drag at the top of the flood. This was another deliberate trap, and we know who it was intended for, this time."

"And therefore all the other times," said Phillipa, who had joined them.

"Very likely," Tony agreed. "Only we'll never prove that. I doubt if we'll ever prove anything. We've only your word for letting out extra chain, Giles. Good enough for us, but not for the natives over here."

"Susan saw me putting it down. I showed her."

"Fair enough. But that wouldn't make any difference to the *gendarmerie*."

"Possibly not. No point in arguing it. We'd better get the anchor in now. God knows where it is, or the chain either."

They soon discovered this. Their chain was firmly wrapped about that of the boat to which they were tied. They dared not pull it free without danger of casting both boats adrift.

"Have to wait for the owners," said Giles. "Better get dressed and see what we can do about those stanchions."

They did not have to wait long. About half-past four a heavy dinghy with an outboard motor put off from the hard and four men came on board the fishing boat.

Recriminations were followed by a long explanation from Giles, patently not believed.

"But don't you understand?" he shouted at last, "if I'd made a mistake over the chain when we came here, and if I hadn't put down more yesterday morning, we'd have floated off yesterday, when we were all at the creek bathing, or rather when we were having lunch at the château. It didn't happen then, so the chain must have been altered some time after that, when the tide had gone down a bit."

Reluctantly the fishermen agreed that this was probably what had happened. They hastened to add that they did not belong to Penguerrec themselves. Giles saw the point of this, and ignored it.

"How do you propose we disentangle the chain?" he asked.

The skipper of the fishing boat had a simple remedy.

"I pull up my chain and when we come to yours, we cut a link, and we are both free."

"And my anchor at the bottom of the river," said Giles. "No, thank you."

He explained his own scheme. They would pull in their respective chains until the tangle appeared and then, from the big dinghy, they could secure his anchor, and sort out the trouble.

"And if we are off the bottom by then?" asked the fisherman.

"We'll have our engines on, which will keep us under control," Giles answered.

After some further argument this scheme was adopted. Giles retrieved his anchor, but they found it necessary to cut his chain in order to free it. Several links had been damaged.

"It is a pity," said the fisherman, politely, "but there was no other way. You will have to have it repaired. And in the meantime . . ." He shrugged, looked at his crew, and added, with a grin, "You had better get out to sea quickly."

Giles grinned back.

"Not before I find out who did the dirty on me," he said.

The other's face hardened.

"That would be a mistake," he said, briefly.

"Why so?"

The man's face went blank.

"Do you start now, at once?" he asked. "I have to go to Tréguier."

"If you can give me ten minutes to rig a line on my anchor, I'll move further in-shore."

The skipper agreed, and even proved helpful to the extent of telling Giles exactly where he could lie to avoid the mooring chains of the other boats and also avoid drying out.

Working fast, Giles and Tony got out the rope they used for the kedge anchor, and reinforced it with another line. Presently they moved away from the fishing boat, and dropped the anchor again.

"It ought to hold in this weather," Giles said. "And it isn't for long."

"Why can't we go now?" Phillipa asked.

"For two reasons. One, that we'll have to go west now to Morlaix, to get the chain fixed, which means we want to use the whole of the ebb, which goes westerly along the coast. Two, that I'm going ashore to have it out with Henry."

He went below, without waiting for an answer, and neither of the Marshalls made any further protest.

Giles's anger festered throughout breakfast, a silent and un-comfortable meal. Then, alone, he set out for the hard.

"You look after *Shuna*," he said to Tony, as he pushed away from her. "I'll look after Henry."

But when he reached the château he found that this was im-possible. For Henry Davenport had disappeared.

CHAPTER IX

HE STOOD ON the doorstep, an incredulous frown on his face.

"*Disappeared?*" he repeated. "Gone out, don't you mean?"

"No, monsieur," Francine answered, coming across the hall to the open door. "Naturally, if he is not in the house, he has gone out of it. But not as you are thinking, for a walk, or even a visit. He has disappeared. We do not know where he is."

The girl who had opened the door gave Francine a frightened look, and hurried away.

"He didn't tell anyone he was going? Not even madame?"

"Not even *me*," said Francine, drawing herself up, her heavy figure presenting the maximum of outraged dignity. "This has never happened before. It is that which makes me afraid."

Her voice broke as she said these words, and looking at her closely, Giles saw that her eyes were red from crying.

"Then perhaps I may speak to Madame," he said, quietly.

"She is in her room," Francine answered. "Mademoiselle Susan is with her. They will not be expecting you. We understood that you intended to leave very early this morning."

"So I did," said Giles, grimly. "And the reason why I'm not half-way to Lézardrieux now needs an explanation—very urgently. I came to get it from Monsieur Henri."

"That is clearly impossible."

There was no answer to this. Giles went towards the foot of the stairs. When he began to go up them, Francine, who had been standing, rigid and silent, near the door, suddenly came to life again and hurried after him.

"I do not know if you can see Madame," she said, in a low agitated voice. "She is beside herself. She imagines things."

He paused, looking back at her.

"Such as?"

"It is ridiculous—absurd. She imagines he has hidden himself in order to frighten her."

"You think that is ridiculous?"

Francine shrugged.

"What else? It is not the conclusion of a sane person."

"What do you consider a sensible conclusion?"

Tears came into her eyes, and began to roll down her cheeks.

"I am afraid for *him*, monsieur."

Giles turned and went on, and Francine followed. He waited while she went into Miriam's room, wondering a good deal about her present anxiety on Henry's account. Before, Miriam had always seemed to be her chief concern.

Francine came out of the room, closely followed by Susan. The old woman watched Giles's face change, and his eyes light up. With a sour look at the pair of them she stumped away downstairs.

Giles caught Susan close to him. They kissed as if they had been parted for twelve months, instead of so many hours.

"You're the only bright spot in this sordid muddle," he whispered.

"Hush! She'll hear us. She's nearly out of her mind. Come in quickly."

The curtains were drawn, the windows all shut. In the half-light Giles saw Miriam, in bed, raised on one elbow, her staring eyes directed towards him, her face haggard and drawn. He went near to her, and could not prevent the convulsive movement with which she flung herself into his arms. Over her head, buried against his shoulder, he looked at Susan. The latter smiled, shook her head in pity and understanding, and crept out of the room.

"Miriam," said Giles, shaking her gently. "Miriam, pull yourself together and tell me what's happened."

His cool voice steadied her. She let go her feverish grip, and lay back on her pillows. Her great dark eyes went round the ceiling, vacant, searching.

"Tell me what has happened," he repeated. "Tell me the truth, as you know it."

That roused her.

"Do you think I would lie to you?"

"I think you scarcely know at present what is the truth and what is false."

She raised herself again on her elbow, and compelled him to look at her.

"You have seen the things that have taken place here. They were Henry's doing. This is the last and cruellest move. He has gone into hiding, on purpose to frighten me to death. He failed to kill me in an arranged accident. Three times he failed. Now he will wait until I can bear the suspense no longer. Until I kill myself, or go mad!"

"No," said Giles. "That's all wrong. I can prove it. Now listen to me."

He told her of the night's events, working up the detail as much as possible, trying to make her think and feel for him and his crew. But he had no success. She had lived too long in the adolescent turmoil of her self-regard.

"You see," he finished, "only someone who understood boats and the sea could have thought of it. Henry understands those things. He must have wanted to get rid of *me*, not you. It all falls into place. You would never have gone down that hole, because you would have noticed the seat had been moved. You often went to see the view from that place, but I was there for the first time. The same with the notice board at the creek. You know the beach there as well as you do the clearing in the woods. I had gone to get the bathing things from the yacht, so it was natural to suppose I would be the first to arrive on the beach. Motive—jealousy. He knew we had been engaged. I grant you, it sounds pretty silly to expect jealousy of that degree in any sane individual, and without obvious new grounds for it. But is Henry a normal person? He has always seemed a bit odd to me."

Miriam moved her tongue across dry lips.

"Susan was with you both times," she said, ignoring his question. "If she hadn't been there, would you really have fallen into the hole? If she hadn't been with you, would you have spent so much time getting the bathing things that Tony and Pip were first on the beach, and Tony was caught in the sand? Did Susan save you from Henry?"

"Perhaps she did, in a way, bless her."

"Are you in love with Susan, Giles?"

"Yes," he told her, quite simply. "I am."

She lay and looked at him.

"In spite of what I told you about her and Henry?"

"Did you tell me anything? If so, I've forgotten, and I certainly don't want to hear it now. It would not be true."

"You are cruel," she said, sorrowfully.

He made an impatient gesture.

"No. No, Giles, don't leave me! Perhaps you are right. Perhaps Henry was trying to get rid of you, not me. Perhaps he was jealous—not for my sake, I assure you—but for Susan's."

"Once and for all, that's nonsense. Fantastic nonsense. You know perfectly well it is false."

"Yes," she said, and her eyes glittered in imagined triumph. "At last you believe me. It is false that Susan has any part in it. I know it is false. Henry wanted to get rid of you and your friends, not because he was jealous of you, but because you were interfering in his plans to bring about my death."

They were back where they had started, Giles thought wearily. She was impossible. Nothing could loosen the grip of her obsession.

He got to his feet.

"Henry often goes off for a few weeks at a time," he said. "You told me so, yourself."

"But he always leaves a note to say he is going, unless he has told me the day before. He never leaves an address, but he does let us know he is going. This time there was no note. He did not even tell Francine."

Giles remembered the old woman had said this, as if it were a great outrage.

"Well," he said. "As Henry isn't here, the less said the better. No good going to the police."

"The *police!*" she exclaimed.

"Why not? I would do just that in England if anyone tampered with my boat in harbour. But it would be no good here. They wouldn't do anything. Except question the fishing types, who'd say it was my own fault for not putting down enough chain. I couldn't prove I had, and that it had been taken up again, and more besides. Whoever did it was cunning enough to leave it as it might have been when I came in five days ago, just after neaps."

A thought came to him.

"Will you be asking the police to find Henry for you?"

Her face sagged. She lay back on her pillows, breathing very fast.

"No," she whispered. "No." Then rallying herself a little she said urgently, "No! Because I don't want him back. Not ever. If only you would take me away, Giles. Save me . . . If only . . ."

She was sobbing and reaching out her arms to him, willing him, forcing him, to share her distress and her fear. But he was utterly wearied; of her, of the whole situation, of his own false position at this moment.

"Go to England, then!" he shouted at her, suddenly losing his temper. "You silly bitch, if you're afraid of Henry, get the hell out of it! There's nothing to stop you. But leave me alone, damn you! I've had enough! I'm leaving the whole bloody business flat, I tell you. Flat."

His violence did not shock her. She enjoyed it. At last she had roused him. She was satisfied.

"You can't leave me flat, Giles," she said, with a little giggle at the word. "Go now, my darling. You will follow this thing to the end. I know it. I will face whatever comes, as bravely as I can. Goodbye and God bless you."

Giles glared at her, speechless, sickened. Then he turned and rushed out of the room.

He was still seething when he reached the hall. Susan was there, waiting for him.

"She's stark, staring," he said. "You'd better get a doctor."

"He's been. But she wouldn't see him."

"Oh, God," he groaned. "That means I can't make you leave this mad-house, I suppose?"

"Not till Henry turns up."

"Do you think he will?"

"I don't think anything. I just hope."

"Write to me. I'll be in Morlaix for a day or two, having repairs done on *Shuna*. Write to me every day."

"Of course I will."

Giles went back to the yacht. The Marshalls were inclined to make light of the new development.

"I don't blame poor old Henry for vanishing," Tony said. "He must lead a dog's life with that woman."

"The point seems to be he always says when he's going away. This time he hasn't. So far."

"Perhaps he was thinking up another of his traps and he's fallen into it himself," suggested Phillipa, hopefully.

"She doesn't like Henry," Tony pointed out.

"He gives me the grues."

"I just never made him out," said Giles. "Until today I was quite prepared to take his word for the traps, as we seem to be calling them."

"You mean that they were set up by village oafs?"

"Yes."

"That would include people who knew about boats, wouldn't it? There can't be many men or boys in Penguerrec who don't know about boats."

"Fair enough," Giles agreed.

Phillipa, who was getting lunch, said, "I know what I'll do. I want one or two stores, so I'll go ashore and have another chat with the grocer's wife. We're great buddies now. I think she likes to unburden herself about the locals. The provincials, she calls them. She was born in Paris. She thinks now that she ought to have settled there, but her parents were very keen on her marrying this grocer. He was a family connection."

"It sounds unbelievably Victorian," said Tony, "but I suppose the system still holds good in places."

"It certainly does. Anyway, I'll have a go at her. She might know something. I suppose it hasn't occurred to either of you two that Miriam might have done away with Henry? That it's been all the other way round, all along?"

"It's an idea," said Tony, thoughtfully. "Traps made to look as if they were for herself, but . . ."

"No," Giles interrupted. "Miriam could never have set the traps. And she's not *pretending* to be afraid. She's half dead with fear."

"She would be," said Phillipa, grimly, "until his body turns up and she knows she's succeeded at last."

"I wonder," said Tony.

A few hours later Phillipa rowed herself ashore. Neither of the men had any errands in the village, and Giles wanted Tony to help him prepare the boat for sailing. So Phillipa went alone.

There were a number of men on the hard, as usual. They eyed her silently, but did not answer her polite greetings. Nor did they offer to help her pull the dinghy up the hard, beyond reach of the rising tide. She had to manage this alone, and was out of breath by the time she had dragged it beyond the fringe of seaweed and found a ringbolt to tie the painter to. She sat down on the harbour wall for a few minutes to recover.

While she was sitting there a girl came along the road and passed her, going down to the hard to speak to one of the men. Phillipa recognised her as one of the maids from the château. She was in ordinary clothes, and Phillipa did not notice her until she heard her voice speaking to the fisherman. She was then aware that the girl, too, had given her no sign of recognition, or even of interest, when she passed her.

So that was that, thought Phillipa. For some obscure reason the village was hostile. She got off the wall and walked slowly up the hill to the main street with its double row of shops.

The grocer's daughter was serving behind the counter. She greeted Phillipa coolly when the latter produced her list. But her enthusiasm for selling was not repressed. She was eager to serve and to find exactly what madame wanted. Phillipa thought regretfully of her usual shopping expeditions at home, where the girl behind the counter carried on a private conversation with her fellow assistant, and was only able to spare a fraction of her time, and no interest whatever, for the customer. But then, of course, the girls at home were not daughters of the proprietor, and the man in charge of the shop did not own it.

The girl weighed out some coffee beans and began to pour them into a bag.

"I wonder if I might grind them here," said Phillipa. "Your mother had the kindness to allow me to use her mill the last time I needed some coffee."

The girl stared, but she went to the back of the shop and called her mother. The latter appeared immediately, and seeing Phillipa, broke into a welcoming smile.

"But of course, madame," she said. "Come in. My little mill is at your service."

Phillipa went into the room at the back of the shop. It was a long, low room, with a bare well-scrubbed kitchen table, and a few upright chairs. The old-fashioned kitchen range stretched the length of one wall. Beside it a huge box was filled with the wood that served it for fuel.

The room was very hot, for the fire was alight in the range, and the window, though open, was small. A cloud of flies buzzed about it and crawled on the table. The grocer's wife drove them away with broad sweeps of her hand, as she brought out her coffee mill and sat down.

"You have been in trouble on your sail-boat," she said. "The men cannot understand it. They thought the English yachtsmen knew how to manage their boats."

"So we do," cried Phillipa, indignantly. "Our anchor chain . . ." Her French did not provide the rest of the explanation. She finished lamely, "Someone made an alteration to it."

The grocer's wife was puzzled, but polite.

"I do not understand such things," she said. "But who could have done it?"

"We do not know."

"You have complained to the police, perhaps?"

"No."

A look of mingled relief and contempt crossed the woman's face.

"Then it is not serious?"

Again Phillipa was nettled.

"I think it is very serious," she said. "But there is some-

G

thing else that is serious. Monsieur Davenport has disappeared."

"*Vraiment*?" said the grocer's wife, calmly.

She filled the top of the coffee mill again with beans and handed it to Phillipa.

"You would like to take a turn," she said. "My hand is tired."

She sat back, complacently watching Phillipa, who set the coffee mill between her knees and began to grind.

"It does not surprise you that Monsieur Davenport has disappeared?" Phillipa asked, presently, as the other remained silent.

"I think it is not exactly true."

"Oh. Why?"

"There has always been a little air of mystery about Monsieur Henri, that is not really true. You understand?"

"No. I'm afraid I don't."

"It is his wife. She is a little queer—*toquée*—you know."

"Mad?"

"Shall we say, not quite normal. It is a misfortune. It keeps him from his friends. I have been told that when she came here first there were scandals. Always young men at the château, and madame seen with them in Paimpol, in Lanion, in Tréguier. Now no one comes here to see her, and they visit very seldom. And then his mother . . ."

She broke off, looked at Phillipa with a considering air, and then went on, "You have heard about his mother?"

"No. His father was English. I know that. He settled here after the First World War."

"Because he had married a Frenchwoman. A Bretonne."

"I see. That was the reason, was it?"

"It was. And then the second war came, and he deserted her."

Phillipa was shocked.

"What do you mean?"

"He went to England with the boy. She did not go. She refused to go."

Phillipa protested.

"But that was not desertion! He was more use, free. I expect he wanted her to go with him."

"She would not leave her country, her people."

This was dangerous ground. Phillipa said, warily, "What happened to her?"

The grocer's wife sighed.

"I do not know, exactly. She went away. The château was occupied. I think she must have died. I did not come to live here until after Monsieur Henri came back from England for the last time. With his English wife."

"I thought he came back during the war?"

"Several times, yes. The people never forgave his father for his desertion. The father died in England, after the war, and they were ready to forgive his son, and welcome him back. But he did not come, until he brought this wife."

"I see. But you told me before that he has many friends among the fishermen."

"That is true. They have always been his friends. That is why I am not disturbed by your news of a disappearance."

"What do you mean?"

The grocer's wife said, in a raised voice, "Voilà, madame! It is finished, our work."

The grocer, a stocky, black-haired man in a wide apron, came through from the shop. He scowled at Phillipa, but said nothing.

His wife poured the rest of the ground coffee into the bag, and getting up, went back into the shop, followed by Phillipa.

The daughter added the coffee to the list of various purchases she had already written down and handed the list to her mother, who turned it round for Phillipa to see.

As the latter handed the money over the counter, the grocer's wife leaned forward and began to whisper rapidly. Phillipa, trying her hardest, both to hear and to understand, was hopelessly lost. But she gathered two words of importance. One was "Henri", and the other was "Roscoff".

"Roscoff?" said Giles, when Phillipa, back on board, had repeated all she remembered of her conversation at the shop. "Henry may be at Roscoff, then?"

"I suppose she could have meant that. Rapid French, in whispers, is beyond me. She definitely wasn't worried about him."

"All right. We're going to Morlaix. Roscoff is quite near there. We'll pick up the trail, if there is one, at Roscoff."

CHAPTER X

Shuna SAILED FROM the Tréguier river at six o'clock that evening. There was no wind in the river, so they had to motor in the first part of the channel. The late sun shone golden on the tall white column of La Corne lighthouse; the tumbled mass of rocks beyond glowed purple and russet in the warm light.

The Marshalls kept exclaiming at the beauty of the changing scene as the yacht drove steadily forward. When they reached the sharp turn in the channel that would take them seawards, they found a little off-shore breeze and hoisted sail. The tide was under them and the wind enough for their purpose, so Giles cut the engine and *Shuna* went on, rising and falling now on the swell that carried her away from the land.

Once clear of the channel and the last barrier of rock, with the shore lights twinkling now far behind them in the blue dusk, they altered course to the west, towards the red afterglow of the dying sun. Tony streamed the log. The wind held, on their beam now, and with genoa set, *Shuna* bowled along at a good pace.

"I'll go inside the Sept Isles," said Giles. "We keep north of Isle Tomé."

He handed the tiller to Tony, and went below to check his course on the chart. Phillipa also went below to get the evening meal. She hoped her sea legs had not deserted her during this harbour-bound week of inaction.

When he had done his calculations, Giles went up into the cockpit again. As he climbed out the light of Les Moines lighthouse on the Sept Isles came on, swinging its powerful beam into the Channel across twenty miles of water.

"Do you see the loom of another light beyond?" he asked.

"I'm not sure."

"Probably not yet. It doesn't matter. We're on course, and we'll see some buoys before long. Once past Tomé, we simply carry on between the mainland and the Sept Isles."

"Triargot was the other light you were thinking of, wasn't it?"

"That's right. We leave Triargot to starboard, too, and go right on towards the Isle de Bas, until we have cleared all the rocks this side of the bay of Morlaix. Then we can go in and find the entrance channel."

"Let's hope this wind holds. We couldn't be more comfortable."

Giles shivered.

"It's getting damned cold."

"Doesn't it always, at night? If you're going below you might chuck me up another sweater, too."

Phillipa was gratified to discover that she was not disturbed by the boat's movement. With the wind so light, and the sea fairly calm, they were not much heeled over, so that cooking was less of a battle than it sometimes was. She produced a good hot meal of soup, followed by stew, previously cooked in the river and now warmed up. This disposed of, they all three sat in the cockpit, letting the fears and shocks and worries of the last few days slide from them, stripped away by the unhurried lift of endless waters under *Shuna*'s hull, and the carved beauty of her sails in the moonlight.

None of them wanted to miss the pleasures of this lovely night, but after a few hours Phillipa's head began to droop and nod, and Tony could not repress his yawns.

"You two had better get some sleep," Giles ordered. "I'll rouse you out if I want you."

"Better have proper watches," Tony suggested.

"I'll see. I couldn't sleep now if I tried, but I'll call you in three hours or so. We'll be there around first light."

Giles was glad to be alone. The last few days had been chaotic. Not only had his past erupted like a cold abscess suddenly incised, but his future, too, had rushed violently at him, demanding recognition. In a revulsion of feeling he was ready to throw up the whole of his tangled responsibilities. He wished he had never gone to Tréguier, or that he had gone creeping up the river in the fog that first morning. Then none of this would have happened. He would never have known that Miriam was up there in the house above the river, with her strange husband, and her even stranger personal conflict. He would never have met Susan, who had unfrozen his heart, so painfully, so completely.

He looked at his boat, lovely on the dark sea. The bright track of the moon glittered beside him, running away towards the mainland, a black shadow, three miles off. On the other side, the long chain of islands, two miles away, glimmered palely. *Shuna* and he were complete in their isolation. Together they harnessed and fought the wind and the sea. Aboard her he lived as he never experienced living on shore, at his job. Except on those occasions, rare and unexpected, when a new idea came to him, some new way of solving a problem in engineering. Those creative moments were exciting. They gave him a sense of power and fulfilment. But this communion with his ship and with the impersonal forces that both sustained and menaced her, went further. It went beyond imagination, inventiveness, all that comprised human brain and human skill, to a far deeper contact, a much fuller comprehension. And how could Susan share in this? How could she break into that region where he and *Shuna* explored together? And if she could not come there, would it not be a betrayal of them all to attempt it?

His thoughts became darker as the night went on, turning more to Miriam than to Susan. His old love's failed marriage seemed somehow to be linked with a failure in himself. And Henry, too, had been betrayed. He went over the events of the last five days. The bitter struggle at the château had both shocked him and confirmed that cynical attitude to marriage he had held from the time of his broken engagement. As the moon dipped towards the west he was amazed to remember the confident way he had determined in his own mind to marry Susan. He scarcely knew her. One girl was very much like another. Thank God he had not committed himself very far.

His thoughts began to run together, in confusion, inconsequent. He invented conversations between himself and Susan, with Miriam and Henry. Checking his course and the log automatically, at intervals, he did not realise how far towards sleep he was drifting, until he heard Phillipa's voice, so loud it seemed to him like a bellow through a megaphone.

"Giles, you're absolutely nodding off! Have some cocoa."

He took the big mug from her gratefully, warming his icy hands against its side, as he sipped the thick scalding fluid.

"Rum in it," he said, hoarsely. "Good girl, Pip."

Tony struggled into the cockpit, shivering as he exchanged the snug atmosphere of the cabin for the chill air above.

"We're hardly moving!" he exclaimed.

"I know. Breeze died about an hour ago. I expect we're going backwards. We were just making against the current when it turned."

"Oughtn't we to do something about it?"

"I didn't want to disturb you two."

"You were practically asleep yourself, you mean?"

"Why not have a break?" Phillipa urged.

"I'll wait a bit and see if we get a puff. There was a suggestion of something from the north-west a few minutes ago."

In half an hour a very gentle air was rippling the water from the north. They re-set the sails and Giles went below. But his drowsiness left him as soon as he lay down on his bunk. He was on deck again long before he was needed to direct the navigation into the Morlaix river.

They anchored at Pen Lann, just outside the river. It had been a slow passage from midnight onwards, and they had too little time left to get up the river and into the lock at Morlaix before the lock gates closed. So they settled down to wait for the afternoon tide, and Giles slept at last, long and heavily. The Marshalls, waking in the middle of the morning, took the dinghy ashore and bathed in the clear water among the rocks.

They reached Morlaix in the late afternoon, and tied up inside the dock. Giles went off at once to arrange for the repair of his anchor chain and stanchions. This did not take long.

"They can't do anything today, but they'll send a chap along early tomorrow morning," he said.

"What shall we do now?" asked Tony.

"Explore," said Phillipa.

"Roscoff," said Giles. "There's a train in half an hour. Electric. We'll dine in Roscoff."

They arrived in the little port just before seven. The station was some distance from the quays, and the road uninteresting until they reached the old part of the town, with its picturesque houses in narrow streets. Giles would not let them linger over these sights, but pressed on towards the harbour.

This consisted of two basins, set parallel with the sea outside, which at this point in the coast ran in a comparatively narrow channel between the mainland and the Isle de Bas.

The larger and more seaward of the two basins held a number of big fishing boats, moored against the quays. These were much larger than any of the craft the three friends had seen in the Tréguier river. The second basin, less well maintained, because, being nearer the land, it dried out for longer periods in each tide, held only small craft, mostly moored to buoys, with "legs" fastened to their gunwales to take the mud and keep them upright when the water had gone. But there was one yacht there, flying a British club burgee at the masthead, and a visitors' French flag at the yard-arm. Giles exclaimed at sight of her.

"I know that boat," he said. "Belongs to an artist chap. Calls her *Palette*, of all unsuitable names for a yacht. What's his name, now? I know—Hurst. Jim Hurst. Met him last year in Audierne."

They went along the high wall of the quay towards *Palette*. Between them and the next basin's quayside there was a low wall on which fishermen were spreading their enormous nets. They looked at the strangers, but did not seem interested. Tourists were expected, and as Phillipa had changed into a summer dress, the visitors wore a very ordinary look.

They found Jim sitting on his cabin top, painting a view of the town across the water. He did not look up as they stopped on the wall above him. No doubt he was used to people staring at him as he worked.

"Hullo, Jim!" Giles called.

That made him turn. He had a deeply bronzed face, shaggy

hair and a beard. He was wearing a very dirty white sweater and cotton khaki slacks. *Palette* had the same scruffy appearance. Her paint was chipped, her varnish faded and worn by sun and salt. She looked as if she had been there for a long time.

Jim laid down his tools on the cabin top and balanced his canvas against the combing of the cockpit.

"Armitage, isn't it?" he said, in a pleasantly deep lazy voice.

"That's right."

"Come aboard."

"Aren't you working? We don't want to disturb you."

"The light's nearly gone. Anyway, I've done enough for one day. Half a sec, I'll fix the ladder."

Palette was tied to the wall along a piece of it that had no ladder, but Jim had his own ladder, which he now lifted against the quayside. They all climbed down. The Marshalls were introduced. Giles asked how long Jim had been at Roscoff.

"A month, about. I shall see the season out here. It's comfortable enough and there are plenty of things to paint."

"I'm sure there are," Phillipa said. "Most attractive things."

She was looking at the unfinished painting in the cockpit. It was purely conventional, a harbour scene, with houses in the distance, and boats in the foreground. But the drawing was firm and the colour clean and true, not prettified.

Jim saw her looking at it, and laughed.

"All commercial," he said, understanding her look. "Posters, travel agencies, the Christmas trade. Gives me a splendid excuse to come over this side for the summer."

"And to run the boat, I suppose?" said Tony. "The best of several worlds."

"Quite."

"Do you sail her single-handed?" Phillipa asked.

"Oh, yes. But I can choose my weather. And I do."

He offered them drinks and Giles invited him to join them for dinner. After a suitable interval the party from *Shuna* left, after arranging to meet in half an hour outside the hotel in the little square behind the church.

"What do we do in the meantime?" Phillipa asked, as they wandered off.

"Go round to the other basin," said Giles.

They walked on in silence.

"That chap said it was comfortable here," Tony began, thoughtfully. "I can't see it, having to look after the boat going down on the sand every twelve hours, and then coming up again."

"Didn't you see he'd got it all taped?" Giles answered. "That pulley with the weight from his masthead keeps him from falling outwards and automatically adjusts his warps. And he had a spar lashed alongside to keep him from scraping the wall, without bothering about moving his fenders all the time."

"His paint isn't exactly worth cherishing, anyhow," Phillipa laughed.

"It takes all sorts . . ." said Giles, easily. "I wish I could speak the patois."

They were standing looking down at one of the fishing boats. There was much activity on board.

"Why? To ask them if they know Henry?"

"Yes. Your grocer friend said Roscoff, didn't she? That he'd gone to Roscoff."

"I *think* she meant that."

"Good enough. I'm afraid it's pretty hopeless, though, just thinking we might run into him."

They left the quay after walking to the far side of the deep basin. Though it was after eight o'clock now, the shops were all open and the little town was still full of sightseers. Giles and his friends walked round the ancient church, admired its curious tower decorated with stone tracery, and turned into the square beyond. They found Jim Hurst sitting at one of the small tables outside the hotel in the corner. He had four tall glasses of golden liquor in front of him.

"I thought you'd need something long after all this walking around," he said, in his deep voice.

"You've already given us drinks," Giles protested. "This was meant to be our show."

Jim laughed.

"You can take over when we get inside," he said. "I'm really very grateful to you for turning up. I like to meet my fellow-countrymen occasionally. I don't see any except trippers as a rule."

He paused to lift his glass to them and then added, "Where's your boat? *Shuna*, isn't she called? I looked in the other basin, but there was nothing English except a motor-cruiser. Bloody great thing like a luxury liner. Just arrived!"

"Must have come in after we left," Tony said. "We saw nothing but fishing boats."

Giles went into the hotel to secure a table. When he came back they finished their drinks quickly and followed him to the dining-room.

There were windows along the whole side of the room that faced the sea. Through these they saw the rocks and the strip of channel and the Isle de Bas beyond. Two big yachts, one Dutch and one English, lay anchored there, white ghosts against the deep blue of the island, their riding lights twinkling like tiny stars above the water.

"That's not *Shuna* out there?" asked Jim.

"No. Twice the size. Actually *Shuna* is in dock at Morlaix."

"*Morlaix?*"

"Look," said Giles. "It's a longish tale and if you're bored, please stop me."

But Jim was not bored, and Giles condensed the story of their visit to the Tréguier river by leaving out nearly all its most important features.

"If you can make head or tail of *that* garbled version, you must be very brilliant," said Phillipa, at the end of it.

Giles reddened, and Jim laughed.

"I gather this man Davenport has hopped it, and that you suspect him of sabotage. Very interesting. You also have a vague clue that he might be in Roscoff. Still more interesting, if not exciting."

"Why?" they all exclaimed.

Diners at the nearby tables looked at them in shocked surprise. Their waiter came to serve them with the next course.

"Because," said Jim, as if there had been no interruption, "I had a few words with a slightly peculiar Englishman very late last night."

"In Roscoff?"

"At the harbour. I was about to go aboard my own boat, to turn in. I was leaning against the wall of the main basin, looking out to sea, watching the lights and the boats leaving the harbour, when I heard a scuffle behind me. I turned round and there were three fishermen holding up a fourth who seemed to be collapsing. I thought he was an ordinary drunk, until they dumped him on a pile of nets and went away. I heard him muttering to himself—in English."

"And then?" Phillipa asked, in an awed voice.

"I went up to him, of course, and asked him, in English, if I could do anything. He pulled himself together at that. Told me he was due on board the *Marie Antoine*, but he was ill, so damned giddy he couldn't stand, and he couldn't see the boat, and they might go without him. The types who had left him there thought he was drunk, though he had told them what he wanted."

"And the boat had gone?"

"No. Luckily she hadn't. In fact they were looking for this chap. Half the crew were up on the quayside, arguing, and calling out for him and to one another."

"Calling him by name?"

"I suppose so. But the Breton dialect is beyond me, except for a few odd words. It wasn't beyond the sick type, though. As soon as we got near, he hobbled away without a word of thanks, and they closed round him and practically lifted him on board, and were off in a matter of minutes."

"That sounds remarkably like our Henry," said Giles. "Just the manners we got. A surly beggar, from start to finish."

"So he's gone fishing," said Tony.

"Oh, no." Jim looked at each of them in turn. "The *Marie Antoine* isn't a fishing boat. She carries onions. This chap was dressed like a typical onion seller, black beret, blue blouse and all. *Marie Antoine* hasn't gone fishing. She's gone to Southampton. She'll be there tomorrow morning, at the latest."

CHAPTER XI

GILES WENT TO St. Malo by train early the next morning. He was lucky enough to find a returned seat on a plane for England, and by the afternoon had arrived in Southampton, booked a room at an hotel there for the night, and set out to find Henry Davenport.

He went first to the docks in search of *Marie Antoine*. This proved more difficult than he expected, until he realised that the Brittany boat had probably left port again. He changed his method of inquiry and soon found that this was so. *Marie Antoine* had docked the day before, discharged her cargo of onions and onion peddlers, taken on board a few stores, and left on that morning's tide.

This was unfortunate. Giles had hoped to find the boat still at Southampton and his task a comparatively easy one. Now he was back where he had started. He was not even certain that the sick Englishman described by Jim Hurst was really Henry. Whoever he was, three things might have happened. He might have gone back to Roscoff on *Marie Antoine*; he might have been well enough to set out with his bicycle and his onions, and be anywhere at all in the southern counties; or he might have landed, been too ill to go on, and be now lying sick in lodgings or in hospital.

Having reached these conclusions, Giles decided that it was not possible for him to investigate any of them but the last. His enthusiasm was considerably damped. He had rushed off from Morlaix without really thinking the thing out. All the way to Southampton he had promised himself a dramatic encounter with Henry, thinly disguised, on board *Marie Antoine*. He might have guessed he would be too late for this. In his own eyes he had lost face, so naturally his resentment against Henry grew.

It was easy enough to get a list of the local hospitals from the main post office. A co-operative clerk told him the most likely one in which to find a sick seaman. But there was no patient there called Henry Davenport.

"Admitted yesterday, some time, I think," said Giles, when the porter at the hospital had gone carefully through the admissions book.

"No, sir. No one of the name of Davenport. No Englishman at all yesterday, as a matter of fact. Two Indians and one Chinese."

A thought occurred to Giles.

"This man was on a Breton boat," he said. "Probably he'd come up with the Breton skipper. They might not be speaking English; most probably wouldn't be. He can talk both Breton and French."

The porter's face lit up.

"A French case?" he said. "Now why didn't you say so before?"

He turned to the girl at the telephone panel behind him.

"Didn't you have a call from Out-patients to transfer a French case to the General?" he asked.

The girl, attracted by Giles's appearance, had been listening to the conversation. She nodded.

"End of the afternoon. Dr. Mathers saw the case in Casualty. We hadn't got a bed in a medical ward here. I transferred it to the Bed Service."

"Do you know what the name was?" Giles asked.

"I don't remember. I'll get E.B.S. for you and inquire."

She pulled out plugs and pushed them into a new formation, and presently was speaking to the telephone exchange of the Emergency Bed Service.

"The name was Henri Dupont," she announced, "and they got him a bed at the General."

"That's right," said the porter, complacently.

Giles thanked them both and left the hospital. Having got so far, even if it proved to be a false track, he decided he must check it. He made his way to the General Hospital, and asked boldly for news of a seaman, Henri Dupont, admitted the day before.

The porter at the General got on to the ward.

"Comfortable, Sister says," he reported.

"Can I see him, do you think?"

The porter looked at the clock.

"Not visiting hours. But you could go up to the ward if you like. You a relative?" he asked, doubtfully.

"Friend," said Giles.

"Well, go along and see Sister. She might be able to help you. He's not on the danger list, or anything like that."

"Good," said Giles, trying to sound relieved.

He was told how to find the ward in question. When he reached it, a nurse made him wait outside, but promised to tell Sister he was there.

Giles began, once more, to feel a fool. Suppose it was not Henry at all? Why the devil should he give his name as Dupont when it was Davenport? The latter could be pronounced in a French way quite easily and would pass as French, if he wanted to conceal his nationality. But why should he? This must be some unknown type, not Henry at all, and he would be justifiably abusive if Giles succeeded in reaching his bedside, only to tell him he was not the man he expected to find.

He was just making up his mind to creep away and disappear, giving up the whole preposterous business, when Sister arrived.

"Do you speak English?" she asked, briskly.

Giles told her who he was, and what he wanted.

"*English?*" she said. "But he hasn't spoken anything but French since he came in with his friends."

"Friends?"

"The men off his ship. From Brittany. He's a Johnny Onions you know." She looked at him, sharply suspicious. "Or don't you know?"

"Look," said Giles, giving in. "I'm trying to find a friend of mine. I think this is the man, but I'm not dead certain. He seems to be using a different name. Can I just have a look at him, to make sure?"

"That's a *very* odd story," said Sister. But there was an amused gleam in Giles's eye, and an air of authority about him that she could not resist. So she led the way into the ward and pulling back the closed curtains of one of the cubicled beds, stood aside for him to look in.

At first Giles thought he had failed. A pale bloated face lay on the pillow, eyes closed. Dark hair, disordered by restless sleep, lay across the forehead. The lips were blue and puffy.

"He is very ill," whispered Sister, "and we don't know yet what is wrong with him. Except this oedema—swelling," she translated.

"They said downstairs he was not on the danger list."

"I think he may be—now," she answered. "The pathologist has just taken a blood sample, and the consultant will be seeing him again this evening. They are really worried."

Giles was still staring. In spite of the astonishing change he decided that this was indeed Henry. When Sister asked, "Is it your friend?" he nodded, and was turning away when the sick man opened his eyes. For a few seconds he glared at Giles, recognition and astonishment plainly shining out, then, deliberately, he shut them again, and turned his head away. But Sister had been watching.

"Five minutes," she said, and went away, closing the curtains behind her.

Giles moved forward and sat down beside the bed.

"I came after you," he said, "to ask you what the hell you meant by tampering with my boat?"

This attack had the effect Giles intended. Henry turned to him with a convulsive movement. His pale distorted face grew scarlet.

"You must be mad!" he cried, hoarsely. "I never went near your boat."

Giles told him what had happened to *Shuna*, and how they had taken her to Morlaix, and picked up Henry's trail at Roscoff. He did not mention the hint they had got from the grocer's wife, only the information supplied by Jim Hurst.

"Yes, he helped me," Henry agreed. There was a bitter note in his voice. "He was about the only one of them who was any use. I've been coming over with the onion boats for years, but they wanted to dump me on the quay and leave me there. They

H

were afraid to take a sick man, they said. I ought to be at home in bed."

"So you ought," said Giles.

"They asked me what to do if I died on board. I said they could put me in the drink and keep their mouths shut."

"You're in a pretty bad way, aren't you?" Giles said, gently.

Henry nodded, struggling up on to one elbow.

"I had to get over here," he said. "If there's any cure for this, whatever it is, I'll get it in this country. Nowhere else."

"What I don't understand," said Giles, "is why you gave a wrong surname and why you've been pretending to speak only French or Breton."

Henry gave him a queer look.

"I didn't want to worry them at home," he said, slowly. "The hospital would have wanted to contact them."

Giles exploded.

"You left without saying a word! Without the slightest warning! You threw the whole household into the father and mother of a panic! Don't pretend you're being considerate. It doesn't go down with me at all."

Henry said, carefully. "I made up my mind rather quickly. I repeat, I did not want to worry them. After all, they know I generally go off on my own about now. They're used to it. I like to meet old friends at Roscoff among the fishing fleet, and so on. We had some exciting times together in the war. And I like to go about Hampshire and Surrey on a bicycle, selling onions. You see the country that way, and all sorts of people. I have no relations to speak of. I don't like Susan's mother, my aunt, you know, and she doesn't approve of me. They never understood my father's settling in France in nineteen-nineteen, nor my mother staying there during the occupation."

He stopped speaking, breathless with the effort and coughing a little.

"Time's up," said Giles, looking at his watch.

"No. Don't go yet. They'll throw you out when they want to. I didn't take in properly what you said about your boat. What exactly happened?"

Giles told him again. He told him he could prove it, because Susan had watched him lengthen the anchor chain.

"Susan," said Henry, thoughtfully.

"I intend to marry her," said Giles. "I hope you have no objection. Not that it makes any difference."

"*I've* no objection," said Henry, smiling for the first time. "Her parents may have, though. She runs their house for them. They're a selfish pair. I told you, I avoid them when I come over. They won't like having to find a paid help, or do the chores themselves."

"They'll have to lump it."

"Is Susan leaving Penguerrec?"

"I wanted her to. At once. I wanted her to go with us."

"But she wouldn't?"

"She wouldn't leave Miriam."

At the sound of that name Henry's face set into a bloated mask, expressionless and grotesque, and to Giles very repulsive in its cold indifference.

He got to his feet, quite determined now to go away and not to come back. But as he watched, he saw a look of entreaty spread over the sick man's features.

"Is there anything I can do for you?" he found himself asking, against his will.

"Two things—yes," Henry panted. He was coughing again and seemed to find breathing difficult. "Go and see my G.P. He doesn't know yet that I am here."

"Your *doctor*, do you mean?"

"Yes. I see him every year when I come over. My slipped disc. He knows my case. Has letters from my Paris specialist. Tell him—get in touch with the people here."

"Yes. Yes, I will, of course. But why not tell the hospital doctors yourself?"

"They think I'm French. I told you. I don't want them to know different."

"You can't keep it up. And if it's only to keep your whereabouts secret, you can't do that, now. I'm going back to Brittany tomorrow, and I shall tell them at the château, at once, where you are and what's the matter with you."

"You don't know what's the matter with me."

This was perfectly true, but it seemed an odd remark coming from Henry, and it was oddly spoken.

"You're ill. That's good enough. The cause doesn't matter."

"It matters very much to me. That's why I want you to see Williams. Dr. John Williams, Ashridge Road, Totton Park."

He stretched out a swollen hand to Giles.

"This may be the end of me, Armitage. I feel awful, and I look awful. The doctors don't know why, yet. They keep talking about allergy and acute rheumatism. But they're wrong. I've been poisoned."

When Giles did not show any startled reaction, Henry repeated, "Poisoned, I tell you. Deliberately poisoned."

He lay still, staring at the ceiling, seeming to forget that Giles was still beside his bed, watching him. Presently he began to mutter, in a low, breathless whisper, "She never loved me. I loved her, but she never really loved me. Never loved anyone. Always changing. But loving herself. Always."

He paused and looked up at Giles. Then he said, clearly, "Bored. Always bored. For years. Wanting to leave me. Now she's getting rid of me. Poison. Miriam has poisoned me."

The vacant eyes closed, and two tears ran out from under the swollen lids, and across the bloated cheeks. Giles crept away.

CHAPTER XII

HE ARRIVED AT Dr. Williams's house just as the evening surgery was beginning. As it was the middle of August, with many people on holiday and no epidemic about, the session did not promise to be a heavy one. Nevertheless he experienced some difficulty in getting an interview with the doctor, who had a justifiable dislike of consultations at second-hand.

By persistence and many-times repeated explanations, however, Giles persuaded the receptionist to add him to the small queue of eight in the waiting-room, on the understanding that he would give up his place to any genuine patient that might turn up later. None such appeared, and Giles, after reading steadily through the back numbers of two popular magazines, was alone in the waiting-room.

Dr. Williams came in person to show him into the surgery.

"You want to see me about one of my patients?" he asked. He did not seem surprised; merely attentive, in a competent, professional way. Giles liked the look of him.

"Yes. I apologise for gate-crashing, but . . ."

"What is his name? Or *her* name?" There was a very slight emphasis on the pronoun. If Giles had been a vain man, which he was not, he might have been gratified.

"Henry Davenport. He sees you about once a year for his back."

"*That* chap!" Dr. Williams got up briskly and went to a small cabinet where his private patients' notes were kept. He found Henry's card and brought it to the desk.

"I'm prepared to listen to what you say, but I don't promise to tell you a single thing," he warned. "Not even if you are a near relative."

"I'm no relative at all."

"Well, go on," said the doctor, glancing at the last entry on the card, then sitting back to listen.

He was a first-class listener, Giles decided. Not absolutely silent, so that you wondered if he were still with you. On the contrary, when you were searching for a way to explain a tricky point, he would prod your mind along with a useful word or two. At the end of it he sat, looking at Henry's record card, turning it over and back and considering.

"You say you aren't related to him? Are you an old friend?"

"No. Not even a friend. A very new acquaintance."

"You did not go to this river on purpose to see him?"

"No."

"Or his wife?"

Dr. Williams asked the question casually, but Giles resented the implication. He was about to explode when the doctor went on, quietly, "You see, he wrote to me a few days ago for an appointment. I was expecting him yesterday. He wrote in his letter that his wife had been very much upset by some yachting people, who had stayed at the château during a storm. So I wondered. You appear to be one of the visitors he meant."

"I see."

This called for a good deal more explanation, of a kind that was not directly any business of Dr. Williams. Giles decided not to give it.

"Henry asked me to tell you where he is," he said, going back to the reason for his call. "He seems to me to be desperately ill, and he thought you could help the hospital doctors with the diagnosis. He thinks he has been poisoned."

"That is quite possible," said Dr. Williams, unexpectedly.

"What d'you mean?"

"The fellow is always taking new so-called cures. He has half a dozen patent medicines with him every time he comes over. A new set each year. Most of them seem to be harmless enough; just the old salicylates got up in a new dress. But last summer he turned up with one of these new drugs."

"Such as?"

"A complicated chemical of the butazolidene type, that does definitely work, at least temporarily. He won't consider an operation, which might cure him. Nor even a supporting jacket. Says it hampers his movements on a boat. So we have to find something to relieve the pain caused by the displaced disc.

We've had this sort of drug in England for quite a time, but I never prescribed it for him, because I didn't feel he was sufficiently under my control. It certainly relieves pain temporarily. Davenport's Paris specialist gave it to him, and warned him, quite properly, against going on with it for more than a week or two at a time, without checks."

"What checks?"

"A blood count, principally. Some people are allergic to it."

This was a word Henry had used. Giles repeated what he had said about himself.

"Then the hospital may be on the right track. He's probably been overdosing himself."

"He spoke as if someone else had been overdosing him, and he'd only realised it when these swellings started, and he began having dizzy attacks. So then he did a bunk, only a bit late in the day."

Dr. Williams looked at his watch.

"Yes," he said. "A bit late in the day. I'll ring the hospital at once. Perhaps you'd like to hear what they have to say."

"Thank you very much."

The hospital had very little to say, but it appeared from the surgery end of the conversation that Dr. Williams was being encouraged to go there and say his piece at a consultation about to take place at the bedside.

He dropped Giles at his hotel on his way to the General. Before they parted, he said, "I think I ought to let his wife know."

"He'll be dead against it. Do you know the address?"

"As a matter of fact, I don't. He never gave me any address. And he always pays on the nail. No National Health Service for him, he says every time. He thinks it's a scandal to provide free treatment and drugs for foreigners. Of course we rather agree in this town. We feel many people nurse their troubles at Cherbourg, to unload them, gratis, on us when they land here."

"Quite."

"Perhaps you can give me the address?"

But Giles had not been lulled into unawareness by the doctor's bland technique of distraction.

"I'll go one better," he said, easily. "I'll tell her myself. I'm going over again in the morning."

Dr. Williams drove off. He knew that Giles had no intention of telling Mrs. Davenport anything at all about her husband. So he concluded that he shared the sick husband's melodramatic suspicion. Well, well, it all made for variety in a mainly drab world. Brittany was a long way off, and he was not in any way responsible for the goings-on there.

Giles got back to Morlaix the following afternoon. Tony and Phillipa were busy polishing the bright work on *Shuna*'s decks. Her wounds had been healed and she looked her smart self again.

"The types were on board all yesterday," they explained, "working like beavers. We can go off again tomorrow, can't we?"

"Look here," said Giles, solemnly, "you two have been simply marvellously patient over this caricature of a cruise. It wasn't my fault we got the fog and the gale. But in a way it was my fault we got mixed up in affairs at the château. I'm damned sorry, but the business isn't finished yet. In fact, I'm up to the neck, now, quite apart from Susan."

He told them what he had been doing in Southampton and finished up with more apologies.

"It wasn't your fault, my dear," said Phillipa, soothingly. "If it was anyone's, it was mine. You didn't want to land on their stage, remember? I made you. And Tony and I are having a wonderful time. We did an extended bus tour yesterday. The country inland is delightful. I wouldn't have missed it for anything."

"Hear, hear," said Tony, polishing hard.

Phillipa dropped her rag and dived below into the cabin, coming up with two letters.

"From Susan, I should think," she said. "We collected them this morning."

She took up her rag again and Giles went below with his letters.

He sat on his bunk, looking at the addresses on the envelopes.

"Giles Armitage, Esq., Poste Restante, Morlaix." The hand-writing on the envelopes was strange to him. He had never seen Susan's writing before. It was a measure of the shortness of their acquaintance, which he was unwilling to acknowledge. She had been so continuously in his thoughts for so many days now, that he had enlarged their friendship and love to un-believable heights of intimacy. But her writing was strange to him.

Reluctantly he tore open the envelopes, looked again at the postmarks to get them in the right order, and began to read.

As soon as he reached the foot of the first page he forgot all about the writing. When he had finished both letters he rushed back on deck.

"Things have been moving in Penguerrec," he told his friends, "and fast, too. Miriam has gone off to Paris. That's in the first letter, so she must have decided to go immediately after we left. Yesterday the police arrived at the château, and they're combing the woods for Henry's body. Susan thinks Francine got them in, but the old woman doesn't tell her anything. We'll have to go back there. Would you mind, terribly?"

"Of course not," Tony answered, and Phillipa nodded agree-ment.

"We don't mind where we go," she said. "Why don't you ring Susan up and go over and see her tomorrow?"

"Bless you both," Giles said.

Susan was delighted to hear his voice. He learned that Miriam was still away and the police were still at the château, turning out all the drawers and cupboards, including those in her own room. But they were perfectly polite and considerate, she said, and had asked her very few questions. There was still no sign of Henry.

Giles passed this over. He did not want to discuss Henry on the telephone. He told her that *Shuna* was ready to go to sea again and that he intended to bring her back to Tréguier at once.

"When will you start?"

"Tomorrow morning, about six from the dock, I think it will be. We shan't get in till after dark, I don't suppose. That's if we can make it on one tide."

"You won't, will you? Why not stop on the way?"

"At Perros, you mean? It's an idea. I could get over from there to Penguerrec tomorrow evening, couldn't I? On a bus, or something?"

"Yes. It would be better than coming here very late, after dark."

She heard him laugh.

"I feel I know the Tréguier river pretty thoroughly now. But you're perfectly right. Anyway, it would make a change for Tony and Pip. They're having a very thin time this cruise, I'm afraid. Though they don't complain."

"Why should they?"

He wanted badly to tell her about Henry. It seemed unfair to leave her in ignorance of the latest development. But if he told her, she would feel bound to send word to Miriam, and until he had seen the police himself and explained to them the whole situation, as he saw it, he did not want Miriam to know that Henry was alive.

So he ignored Susan's last question and said, simply, "I can't wait for tomorrow evening. Take care of yourself, darling. Good night."

He hung up, and walked back to the dock with her answering endearment echoing in his heart.

Giles arrived at the château the next evening. Francine opened the door to him.

He found her very much changed, even in the three days since he had last seen her. Then, she had been suffering from the sudden shock of Henry's disappearance. Now she seemed to have accepted disaster in a mood of dull despair. Her former, confident air of authority had gone, and with it her neat well-preserved appearance. She looked an old woman, and a slovenly one at that. Giles was considerably shocked.

He inquired first for Susan.

"Mademoiselle is in her room," Francine told him.

"And Madame? I was told she is in Paris. Has she come back yet?"

Francine clasped her hands in a sudden access of emotion.

"Oh, monsieur!" she wailed. "If only you had taken her away! If only you had understood her need, and taken pity on her! We are afraid for her. She is not at the address she gave."

"Don't tell me she's disappeared as well!" he cried, in exasperation. "That really would be the end!"

Francine looked at him with hatred in her dark eyes. "You have no heart," she said, bitterly. "I will see if Mademoiselle is allowed to speak to you."

This roused some alarm in Giles.

"What d'you mean by that?" he asked, quickly.

But Francine would not tell him. To punish him for his hard-heartedness she took him to the library, showed him in, and still without speaking, shut the door on him.

"She's going round the bend, too," he thought, gloomily. "What's the matter with this hellish place, to unhinge the lot of them?"

But he decided to humour Francine, for he saw clearly that there was no other way of managing her. A few minutes later the door opened again, and Susan was in his arms.

He knew at once that something had upset her badly, and before long he heard the latest developments. Miriam had sent a long statement to the police in which she accused Susan of contriving Henry's death. The motive was stated to be jealousy. The girl, according to Miriam, was madly in love with her cousin. He had responded to this passion and promised her he would get rid of his wife. Having failed in this, Susan, according to Miriam, became furious. She saw that he was half-hearted, that he would never leave his wife. So she had destroyed him.

"Did you ever hear such fantastic nonsense?" Susan said. "But the police inspector was here all the morning."

Her voice quavered. It had been a day of hideous surprise and strain, and the relief of having Giles with her at last nearly broke her resolution.

"Of course it's ridiculous," said Giles, steadily. "But altogether in keeping with her extraordinary character. They can't really believe a word of it."

"I don't know. The inspector told me he had tried to get in

touch with Miriam at once after he got the statement, but she seems to have left Paris."

"That was worrying Francine, too," said Giles.

"Poor old thing. It's Henry she's chiefly upset about."

Giles could no longer keep his secret. He was going to find the police directly after he had reassured Susan. All the same, he made sure there was no eavesdropper at the door before he told her, in a lowered voice, that Henry was alive and in England.

She was utterly bewildered.

"Then nothing makes sense," she said, faintly.

"On the contrary, I think we've got a very considerable case against Miriam. And this latest ridiculous attack on you only helps it along."

"Poor thing. You mean, she tried to kill Henry, because of her imaginings about him? Like a little girl inventing romantic melodrama, with herself as heroine?"

"Little girls of thirty-two can be dangerous, it seems."

"You'd better see Inspector Renaud at once, hadn't you?"

"The sooner the better. Come with me."

"I'm not supposed to leave the château. So he said this morning."

Giles was furious.

"Francine hinted at something of the sort. It's preposterous. Where is the man, anyway? Where shall I find him?"

"I don't know. We could ask Francine."

The old woman was able to help them. Two uniformed police, she said, were guarding the château. They might know where Inspector Renaud could be found.

"*Guarding* the château?" Giles repeated, incredulous. "What for? What against?"

But Francine would make no suggestion. She merely gave him a stony look, and walked away.

Giles got in touch with the inspector at last, very late that evening, in Tréguier. He told him everything he knew, from the time of his first visit to the château. He told him about discovering Henry in Southampton, and about the probable cause of his illness. He finished by asking what the hell they meant by ordering his fiancée not to leave the house.

"Your fiancée?" asked Renaud, with raised eyebrows. "Tiens!"

He considered Giles for a few seconds, and then said, "She told me nothing about that."

"Why should she?" Giles did not add that he had not had time yet actually to fix the matter. "The point is you have no possible motive for restraining her actions."

"Oh, yes, we have. And perhaps now you have explained your position in regard to her, I can tell you. It is for her own safety."

Giles stared. The inspector went on, in a gentle explaining voice. "We are not so stupid, monsieur, even in Tréguier. And now we have the advice of the Sûreté. You see, we already know where this Monsieur Davenport is staying. We have known for two days. It was reported to us by the skipper of the *Marie Antoine*."

Of course, thought Giles. What a fool I am. The fellow's own friends were naturally anxious about him. And in all probability Henry had also told them his suspicions about the cause of his illness.

"We have daily reports of his progress," Renaud went on. "He does not improve. He may die. Either during the next few days, or, if he survives this period, in a year or two from now. We are waiting for the immediate news."

"But you have not told his wife? Or have you? You have not told anyone at the château."

"It is not necessary to tell anyone at the château."

He looked straight at Giles, who stared back, considering this ambiguous statement.

"Do you mean, they know? But I'm sure they don't. Or didn't, earlier today. Naturally I told Susan, Miss Brockley."

"Naturally," repeated the inspector, softly.

"Are you telling me Francine knows, and the maids know, and kept it to themselves?"

"I am not telling you anything."

"Very well," said Giles, stiffly, getting to his feet. "I'm

sorry I came. You know it all already, and I can be of no use to you. But I shall see the nearest British consul tomorrow about your treatment of Mademoiselle Brockley."

Inspector Renaud also rose to his feet.

"If what you tell me of your relations with Mademoiselle is true, then it is indeed necessary to protect her. But are you correct in what you say? It would be natural for her to mention this important fact when I was questioning her about your former engagement to Madame Davenport. She did no such thing. I ask myself if you invent it for your own protection."

"Do you, indeed? I see."

Giles saw, only too clearly. Henry had obviously put forward his suspicions of his wife. Someone, perhaps Susan, in her innocence, or Francine, who seemed to blame him for not championing Miriam, had explained his earlier tie. The logical French mind, used besides, to strong emotional reactions, would conclude, accurately enough, that Miriam, out of love with her husband, might wish to renew that tie. It would not seem altogether strange to this inspector that she might try to poison her husband; or even that Giles might be willing to help her.

Watching Renaud Giles was sure he regretted the further complication of Susan's presence in all this. As a man of the world he could accept Giles's fresh attachment, but he found it tiresome, all the same, and an added responsibility. Which must mean that he agreed with the possibility of Miriam's guilt.

"You think Madame Davenport did poison Henry, don't you?" Giles asked him. "And might go for Susan, now. If so, why don't you arrest her?"

"First, because I do not know where she is," answered the inspector, suddenly abandoning his official manner. "And second, because I expect her to come back to Penguerrec. They always return."

He uttered this platitude as if it were a new discovery of his own, with a return of his former pompous authority. But seeing the gleam of amusement in Giles's expression, allowed himself to laugh softly.

"Eh bien," he said, leading the way to the door. "It is no good trying to impress an English yachtsman. They are all stubborn and reckless; a terrible combination."

"I am never reckless—I hope," said Giles, piously.

"You must not be so in this case," the inspector told him, solemnly. "It is important that you keep your mouth shut. Madame Davenport is not to know that her husband lives. Not yet. No one is to know. Mademoiselle Brockley must tell no one."

"She promised to keep it secret until I had seen you. But if Francine knows, and all the village . . ."

"Madame Francine is very discreet. The girls obey her."

"What will you do next?"

"Wait, monsieur. I have no evidence of attempted murder. Or of any other crime. There has not, so far, *been* any murder. Therefore I must wait. We must all wait."

CHAPTER XIII

MIRIAM ARRIVED BACK at the house the following morning, in a hired car. The driver carried her two suitcases into the hall and put them down, looking about him nervously. He had heard about the situation at the château. His wife had read him an account that morning of the disappearance of this Monsieur Davenport. The facts were meagre, but several interesting theories were put forward. When he was engaged at the railway station to take the lady to the château, he felt quite excited. He did not know who she was, but he thought it would be amusing to see the place. Now he was regretting his enthusiasm. It was not at all amusing.

In the first place he had been surprised and a little alarmed when a gendarme came out of the bushes beside the closed main gates, and asked him what he wanted. It did not help to re-assure him when Miriam, lowering the window of the taxi, declared that she was the mistress of the place, and demanded to be allowed in immediately. After that the gates were opened, with no delay and no further questions. But the taxi driver had been quite startled by the incident.

The atmosphere of the grounds had done nothing to lessen his forebodings. His wheels bumped over the uneven, weed-grown surface of the drive; the overhanging trees in places scraped the roof of the car. He felt profoundly depressed. The newspaper had used the word "sinister" in connection with Davenport's disappearance. He felt this was completely justi-fied.

His opinion was confirmed when he carried Madame's suit-cases into the deserted hall. She had opened the door herself, simply by turning the knob. So it was not locked. But the house seemed to be deserted. There was no one in the hall when he followed her in with the luggage. No one came in response to the noise of their arrival. The only sounds in the house were of their own making. He felt scared, and it did not help him to notice how pale Madame had become in the subdued light of that silent hall, and how hurriedly she found her purse and paid him for his services. He drove away convinced that the newspaper had understated, rather than exaggerated, the case.

When he had gone Miriam shut the door and stood for a minute inside it, listening. A faint sound from above came to her. She looked up quickly, and saw in the shadows of the first landing the white face of the younger of the two maids.

"What are you doing there, Marie?" she called, sharply, and was infuriated by the girl's quick gasp of terror. "Why didn't you come down at once when you saw me arrive?"

Marie moved reluctantly to the head of the stairs. Miriam saw another shadow behind her, Francine. Had she been there all the time, as well?

"Do as Madame orders," Francine said, clearly.

"Oui, madame," the girl answered, but she moved forward with obvious reluctance.

Francine waited until Marie reached the hall, then turned quietly and walked away.

Miriam watched her go, furious at her polite neglect. She told the girl brusquely to take her suitcases upstairs, then turned and went into every room in turn, finding each one empty, silent, accusing.

Having visited all of them she went back to her own sitting-room, and flung herself into a chair. The uncertainty and dread she had experienced since Henry's disappearance had returned to her in full force. Francine's behaviour, little Marie's hesitation and awkwardness, the police at the gate, all menaced her. Every desperate struggle she made only seemed to enlarge her danger. She was near breaking point, and she knew it. If only Susan would come and talk to her. Where was she, anyway? Surely the police . . .

Presently the door opened, and Susan came in. Miriam sprang to her feet.

"Hullo!" she said, unsteadily. "You startled me."

"Why?" asked Susan. "Did you think I had been arrested? Was that what you intended?"

Miriam's mouth went dry.

I

"I—I don't understand," she managed to say.

"Oh, yes you do. Inspector Renaud told me what you reported to him. Every detail of every lie, it sounded like."

"How dare you?"

"Don't be utterly silly. Of course I dare. You invent a string of lies about me, the police don't allow me to leave the house, and you have the nerve to grumble if I accuse you of it. Really!"

Miriam sank back into her chair and put her hands up to her eyes.

"I didn't mean to hurt you," she said, faintly. "I have never meant to hurt anyone. I have only tried to save myself—from Henry."

"Hush!" said Susan, as Inspector Renaud came into the room.

Miriam took her hands from her face, and lay back in the chair, staring up at him. Susan moved towards the door, and at a nod from the inspector went through it, closing it softly behind her.

"So you have returned, madame?" said Renaud, looking sternly at her.

"Yes, I have returned."

"I am curious about three things, madame. Why you went away, so secretly, and so immediately after your husband vanished? Why you informed us, *after* you had left, that he had disappeared, and you were afraid he was dead? And why you hinted, very openly, that Miss Brockley might be responsible?"

Miriam sat looking at him for some time, quite obviously arranging her explanations before giving voice to them. Inspector Renaud was patient. He knew from his inquiries that he had to deal with an hysterical woman. Her present calm was deceptive, he guessed. He was anxious not to break it before he had heard what she wanted to tell him.

"I was wrong about Susan," Miriam said, at last. "I was distracted. I lost my head. You must understand that my husband was always difficult. He used to go away by himself, not telling me where he went. Naturally I concluded . . ."

She looked at the inspector, who nodded gravely. He would come to the same conclusion, he decided.

"So I was anxious when he asked this attractive girl, his cousin, to come here. It was his invitation, not mine. I did not know how well he knew her, or how often he had seen her. I was meeting her for the first time, but he . . ."

She looked at the inspector again, and again he nodded his agreement with her unspoken suggestion. But this time he spoke.

"If, as you suggest, there was a liaison between Monsieur Davenport and Mademoiselle Brockley, I do not understand why she should want to murder him."

"Because he had failed to murder me," said Miriam, quite simply.

As Inspector Renaud made no answer to this, she went on, "You have heard of the various traps that were laid for me?"

"I have heard of the—incidents—but I have not yet found a satisfactory explanation."

"You don't believe that Henry was trying to kill me?"

Renaud looked severe.

"It is I who make the inquiries, madame," he reminded her. "And I am investigating the fate of Monsieur Davenport. You, madame, are very much alive."

He smiled at her, and feeling warmed and encouraged, Miriam smiled back, and lowering her voice, said confidingly, "I hope I may have misjudged poor Henry. As I said at first, I no longer think Susan was responsible. After all, whatever may have been between her and Henry in the past, she seems to have transferred her affection now to another Englishman."

"Ah," said the inspector. "Monsieur Armitage, you mean?"

"Then she has told you about him?"

"Not exactly. Monsieur Armitage was very definite, though."

That shook her.

"But he has gone! He told me he was going!"

"He has come back."

"Come back? . . . Then he could not leave things as they were! . . . He had to know . . . He came back to . . ."

Renaud could see her mind beginning to work out a new set of possibilities, a new combination of suspicion and accusation,

involving this time, not Susan, but Giles, her own former
lover. The obvious, frantic rushing hither and thither of her
thoughts affected the inspector strangely and most disagreeably.
His own ideas about Giles were shaken by her shameless, false
devising. Where he had expected to see his theory passionately
rejected by a guilty woman, he saw it blossoming in an imagination so unhealthily fertile that he was shocked, hard-bitten
policeman that he was. He was shocked, too, to find how moved
he had been, a little earlier, by the sweetness of her smile when
he had told her she was very much alive. Such beauty had to be
alive. Unthinkable that it could be lost. But how terrible to find
it enclosing a mind so feverishly corrupt. How unusual, how
confusing. How unlike his own countrywomen, thank God.
But all the more reason to be careful, and unyielding, and cold.

He took himself firmly in hand.

"We will not, at this moment, discuss Monsieur Armitage,
either," he said. "You will tell me why you went to Paris, and
what you did there."

She responded at once to the change in his manner. Now she
was quiet and reasonable; a sensible wife, concerned for her
husband's health.

"I went to see his doctor," she explained. She continued
with a long explanation of Henry's illness, most of which
Inspector Renaud already knew. He did not interrupt her. This
apparent frankness on her part might be very useful. At last it
showed him just how much she knew about her husband's
condition.

"For weeks I have seen him getting worse," she said, with
just the right note of tender solicitude. "Last year his hands, or
rather his fingers, were swollen for a few weeks in the winter.
Now this summer they have been getting worse all the time,
and not only the fingers but the wrists and ankles as well.
There were times when he could not wear shoes, but only
carpet slippers, and other times when he could not pull on his
fisherman's rubber boots. That made him absolutely furious.
Quite apart from his back. He will not wear a support for the
slipped disc, you know. But the worst thing was the heart
symptoms."

"The heart?"

"He had fainting attacks. It was really over this that I went to Paris when he disappeared. He had never allowed me to discuss his case with his specialist. Our local doctor never attended him. He used to call him in to see me, occasionally. But really, I am never ill."

She said this gaily, with another of her breath-taking smiles. Inspector Renaud took an even firmer grip on his feelings.

"What did this specialist tell you?" he asked, and added, "I should like to have the name and address, please."

She gave them and went on, "He told me that Henry's heart was absolutely sound, that he had not seen any sign of a worsening of the disease at the last examination."

"When was that?"

"Three weeks ago. We went to Paris together three weeks ago and Henry had his consultation the next morning."

"Only one consultation?"

"Yes. Then we stayed on to see one or two plays and do a little shopping. We came back . . ."

"I know that part of the story. It is where everything begins, isn't it?"

"Yes."

She looked at him very gravely, her long dark eyes sad, but resigned now, it seemed, to Henry's fate.

"I still do not understand your own visit to Paris this week, madame."

"Don't you see? I had only heard from Henry about his illness. Never, until now, from the doctor, himself. I wanted to know particularly about his heart, on account of these fainting attacks, this recurring dizziness. Can't you understand? I thought he might have fallen from a height, or into the river."

"And you went all the way to Paris to discover if this was likely to happen?"

"Yes. To know if he had been warned about his heart."

Precisely, thought the inspector. If he had been warned that his heart was affected, and his body should turn up at last on some beach nearby, where the conflicting currents had thrown it, natural causes would explain the death, added to Henry's foolhardiness in boats.

"So you discovered, contrary to your expectations, that Monsieur Davenport's heart was sound?"

"Yes."

"This specialist could offer no explanation of the symptoms you had noticed recently?"

"Only one. That Henry had been taking too much of his new drug."

"Ah," sighed the inspector.

It was a sign of admiration, quite as much as an acknowledgement of defeat. This was counter-attack on the grand scale, and made with such superb confidence that he almost began to wonder if Henry were lying, instead of his wife.

"And what did you say to that?" he asked, eager for her next move.

The big soft eyes filled with tears.

"That it was only too possible. He had been warned against it, against taking too much for too long. He was always taking things, answering advertisements, trying the old-fashioned concoctions Francine brewed for him . . . everything. He believed that the more you took, the better the effect. He would not try to understand these modern drugs which are so different."

She paused, but as Renaud said nothing, she went on, boldly, "I tried to check him. I sometimes hid the tablets in a drawer in my room. Then he had to wait until a fresh lot was sent. It meant a few days' respite. At the last I found the prescription and hid that, too. You will find it with some tablets in my room."

"We have already found them, madame."

Her eyes widened, but she only said, "Then you know that you can believe me."

Inspector Renaud got slowly to his feet. In his twenty years as a police officer he had questioned many suspects, but never before had an apparent lie looked so much like the truth. Her explanation was so simple, so very convincing. But he remembered that it was not her first. There had been that confused accusation, levelled at the English girl.

"It depends," he said. "If you had told me this story at once, perhaps. But why did you leave your hotel in Paris and remain hidden for twenty-four hours? Where did you go for this period of time? What were you doing? And why did you accuse Mademoiselle of doing away with your husband, if you had already made up your mind that he had recklessly overdosed himself with his medicine?"

She looked utterly confused. She stared at him as if he had accused her of ideas and actions she had never even thought of. Then, as before with Susan, she covered her face with her hands, and broke into loud sobs.

"I—I was mad to say that!" she cried, at last. "I was so confused. Dreadful things had happened . . . Giles . . . Susan . . ." She controlled herself with a great effort. "We shall know all when you have found his body," she said, striving for dignity.

"We shall, indeed," said Renaud.

Miriam collapsed again, crying bitterly.

"You are upset," said the inspector, unnecessarily. "We will talk again another time."

All his sympathy had melted, washed away by these excessive, childish tears. She was not any longer beautiful, fascinating, mysterious. She was repellent.

"I will send Mademoiselle to you," he said, and strode out of the room.

Miriam stayed where she was, sunk in her chair, sobbing quietly into her handkerchief. She was not crying for Henry, or for her sins. She was lamenting her own failure, her own crass ineptitude.

CHAPTER XIV

IT WAS NOW a week since Henry had left his home, and five days since his admission to the General Hospital at Southampton. Contrary to all the doctors' expectations, he was improving steadily. The oedema that had affected his lungs as well as his extremities had not turned to pneumonia as they had all feared. The swelling of his hands and feet was going down; his face was returning to its normal outline. The salt content and mechanism of his body, thrown out of gear by the overdose of the drug he had taken, was returning to normal. In fact, as the house physician explained to him, he had had a very lucky escape, and it had been a very near thing. It was up to him to have more sense and do what he was told about his medicines in future.

For the hospital staff were not aware of the complicated background to his case. As soon as the French police got in touch, through Interpol, with the C.I.D. in Southampton, Dr. Williams was warned to keep his mouth shut at the hospital. He had been discreet enough, for he had not believed Henry's statement that he had been deliberately poisoned. He agreed with the hospital consultants that the man was an eccentric who had overdosed himself.

The theory was not upset by the arrival at the General of a plain-clothes officer to see Henry. The object of his visit, he stated, was to check the man's passport. This seemed very reasonable, as they had accepted him under the name of Henri Dupont, and the passport he produced when admitted was in that name. There was clearly something a bit fishy about the man whom Dr. Williams knew as Henry Davenport.

In point of fact, Henry had two passports. The French one had been faked for him in the war, together with the other necessary papers of his assumed character, when he was passing backwards and forwards between Brittany and Plymouth. This had been done so well that he was able to renew it without difficulty when the war was over, and had kept it up to date for use on his summer trips. But he had, besides, an English passport in his own name, which he also carried with him-on his visits to England, to prove his nationality if the need arose. The Southampton police sergeant sorted out this interesting information, but was unable to do anything about it. Apart from the assumed name on the French one, both his passports were in order. And the foreign one had been issued by the French authorities; it was not a forgery. But the position was sufficiently unusual to make the sergeant less sympathetic with Henry's illness. The chap was probably a shady character, anyway. In the atmosphere of a great port, smuggling was always present in the minds of the police. Perhaps the onions were only a cover-line.

These suspicions, though vague, were reinforced when Henry decided, a few days later, against advice, to go home. Southampton was sure now that he had been up to no good. The fact that he had nearly died of poisoning was beside the point, in the sergeant's view, and that of his superiors. Reluctantly they informed their opposite number in France. Henry was put in touch with Inspector Renaud; the confrontation plan was explained to him. The date for this was arranged two days ahead, when the *Marie Antoine* would arrive back from Southampton after her next call there. Henry was advised to make contact with the boat at once, and secure a passage in her. He did so, and left the hospital the same day. They were sorry to lose him, because he had been an interesting case, and was not yet completely cured. They made him sign the usual form handed to patients who take their own discharge against medical advice, and the house physician saw him into a taxi at the front door of the hospital. He went aboard the *Marie Antoine* that evening, and she sailed at midnight.

Meanwhile Giles had taken *Shuna* back to the Tréguier river. He avoided the landing-stage, dropping his anchor just outside the cluster of fishing boats, on the side of the little anchorage near the mouth of the creek, but out of the main current that swept through it on the tides. This was some distance from the hard, but he was unwilling to use the landing-stage any longer. He wanted to confirm his independence of the house above the river. If it had not been for Susan he would never have allowed himself to become embroiled there again.

Having got back to Perros late at night on the day before, he had felt too tired to make the very early start necessary to work the first tide of the next day. Since the harbour at Perros dried out, he would have to wait until at least half-tide on the flood before leaving. This would leave very few hours in which to get into the Tréguier river, though the stream would be with them along the coast when they reached the eastward side of the Isle Tomé. With a good breeze it could be done comfortably, but a fresh anticyclone had arrived, with cloudless skies, bright sun, but very little wind. So he decided to make a day of it, escaping from Perros just in time before *Shuna* took the ground. It was a pleasant meandering day of drifting about, taking advantage of any little puff that came; making his way, in a most leisurely fashion, out to sea during the morning, and back towards Tréguier in the afternoon. It was evening when they arrived.

Giles rowed ashore at once to telephone to Susan from the post office. She told him that Miriam was back.

"How is she?"

"Worse than ever. Lashing out at everyone, and then crying over the way she is being treated."

"Who by? Not you, surely?"

"Inspector Renaud. No, she has taken back the lies she told him about me. Really, I don't think she knows what is the truth and what isn't. I think she believes everything she says as she goes along."

"I think that was always the way of it."

He paused, remembering so many occasions when that must have been true, and his younger self had been lacerated, not understanding her strange self-torturing nature.

"Hullo," Susan said, wondering if he had hung up.

"I'm still here. Darling, I must see you. The sooner the better. Is the nonsense still on? I mean, can you leave the house?"

"The house, yes. Not the grounds. And not even the house, at night. It'll have to be tomorrow morning."

"Then look. We'll come along, all three of us, round about ten. Be down near the main gates, but not near enough to worry the gendarmerie into thinking you are about to break out. Then Tony and Pip can go on up to the house, and we can go off down to the creek. I've a lot to say to you. Very important."

Her voice was low, but quite steady as she answered, "Yes, Giles, I'll be there."

"Good girl. 'Bye for now."

He walked back to the hard, feeling calmer. All that day his pleasure in sailing had been overlaid by vague fears for Susan. Inspector Renaud was so obviously on the warpath, so determined to make something of the unusual opportunity that had come his way. And he had a most perplexing set of facts to sort out. No wonder he had been ready at first to jump to any easy conclusion that presented itself.

However, Susan's report must mean that the inspector was now exercising his common sense and native shrewdness. He was no fool, Giles had already discovered. He might want to employ the usual Gallic methods, and who should blame him for that? This business of bringing Henry back in secret might appear crude and old-fashioned to British eyes, but it was really no cruder than the verbal equivalent, the sudden unexpected question, the sudden production of a piece of evidence withheld until the suspect was at the point of breakdown. Well, they would have their confrontation, and Miriam would undoubtedly throw a fit. And where did Renaud go from there? What exactly would he have proved? What exactly was there to prove?

It was a hideous business altogether, Giles told himself. Miriam thought her husband was trying to kill her. Henry thought his wife had poisoned him. Which of them was right, if either? Or were they both right? Henry had been convinced, telling his story painfully from his bed in Southampton. Miriam could point to the strange accidents that might have taken her life, and which she was sure were directed to that purpose. She had a case, though it was not altogether clear. So had Henry. Neither of them had any real proof against the other. Would the whole thing peter out, as far as the law was concerned? Would they have to continue together in that fear-ridden house, with those strangled crimes lying between them?

Giles rowed back to *Shuna* from the hard, feeling more utterly depressed than ever before in his life. The cruel outline of the rocks at Pen Paluch was starkly black against the green afterglow of the sunset. There would be a late moon, and the light was fading fast.

Even the warmth and comfort of *Shuna*'s cabin, and Phillipa's excellent supper, failed to raise his spirits. The others asked for news of Susan, but did not pursue the subject. They made no objection when Giles decided to turn in early, but meekly took to their own sleeping-bags, and while he lay in darkness in his quarter-berth, making no sign that showed whether he were awake or slept, they read silently for a while, and then turned out the lights over their heads, and settled down for the long night, which Phillipa, at least, welcomed with joy.

At about two in the morning, in a night lit by the gibbous moon, with the river motionless at slack water on the ebb, *Marie Antoine* slid quietly to a berth off Penguerrec. She moored between two buoys provided for the use of larger vessels entering the river, and some three hundred yards from *Shuna*. No one saw her arrive except Inspector Renaud, shivering in a greatcoat on the hard beside the sea wall.

But Giles saw her go. He slept fitfully, and woke, as usual, at first light. Hearing the noise of engines and men calling to one another, he went up into the cockpit. He saw the onion boat cast off from the buoys, and as she turned to go down the river to the sea, he saw her name on her stern. It was cold on deck; the morning air struck at his body through his thin pyjamas. But a deeper chill froze his heart. He went below again, but not to sleep. He rightly judged that the show-down at the château was on, and he dreaded the outcome. But his voice, when the others woke up a few hours later was quiet, even casual, as he told them, "Henry's back."

"No!"

Phillipa, lighting the gas under the kettle, burned her fingers on the taper in her excitement.

"Ouch! You shouldn't say these things, Giles, when I'm getting breakfast."

"Sorry. I thought you'd like to know."

"Did you see him?" Tony asked. "How did he come? When?"

"I saw very little. Only the backside of *Marie Antoine*, when she slipped her moorings this morning, early."

"She wasn't in last night when we went to bed."

"Exactly. I imagine she got here at low water or just after. So she can't have stopped more than a couple of hours. Just time to disembark Henry, I expect."

"You don't actually *know*, then, that he came on that boat?" Phillipa said.

"Inspector Renaud told me she was bringing him over. She'd be due just about the time she did, in fact, put in here. On her way back to Roscoff, I suppose. Renaud wanted it all kept dark. Well, it was. Very dark."

"I wonder where he is now?" Tony said, thoughtfully.

"We'll soon find out," Phillipa put in. "It can't be kept from Miriam for ever. Besides, isn't the idea for him to turn up suddenly and surprise her into admitting she tried to poison him?"

"That is Inspector Renaud's theatrical intention," agreed Giles. "Now listen. We're all going to the château this morning. Susan is going to be down by the gates, waiting for us. I hope we'll get through the gendarmerie all right. Then I want you two to go on up to the house, and talk to Miriam, while I go off with Susan for a little walk."

"Yes," said Phillipa, with full understanding.

They went ashore just before ten o'clock. There was a brief argument with the guard at the gates, but with Susan's arrival, almost at once, the opposition collapsed.

"Inspector Renaud knows me," Giles insisted, for the tenth time.

"I am aware of that, monsieur. The inspector has given

orders that no stranger or visitor shall be admitted this afternoon. He made no rule for this morning."

"Then we can go to the house?"

Reluctantly, the man agreed. They all walked up the drive together until they were out of sight of the gate. Then they stopped.

"So the balloon goes up this afternoon," said Giles, grimly.

"I think we ought to warn her," Phillipa burst out. "It's a shocking way to treat her."

"What is?" Susan asked.

Giles explained. The girl's face whitened.

"What would happen if we did tell her Henry is alive?"

"We should all be run in for obstructing the police in the performance of their duty," said Giles. "I haven't the slightest doubt of Renaud's reaction. This is his big moment. If we baulk him of it, he'll have our blood, the lot of us."

"I'm quite sure she did try to do Henry in," Tony said. "I'm for not interfering."

"But it's so heartless," Phillipa insisted. "Couldn't we harp on the fact that his body hasn't been found, and we, personally, think he may be alive? She's sure to talk about it. I suppose it's her guilty conscience makes her so sure he must be dead."

"Are we really certain he *is* alive?" asked Susan. "He left the hospital, I suppose, if Renaud said he was on the way back. But he was very ill, wasn't he, Giles? He may have died on the voyage, or anything. I mean, we don't *know*, do we? It would be safer not to tell her anything."

Giles put an arm round her and drew her away.

"None of us really knows anything," he said over his shoulder, to the others. "We've done a lot of guessing, but haven't got many hard facts. And after all, Miriam called in the police herself, remember. It's up to her, now."

"All right," Phillipa said, as she and Tony moved away. "I don't like it. I feel very much like warning her. I'd really rather not see her at all. I'm only doing it for you, Giles. I hope you're grateful."

"Deeply," he said, and made a face at her. She hurried off to catch up Tony, who had walked on.

"I don't think you need be too sensitive about our position," Tony said, "unless and until a crime has been committed. It hasn't been proved yet that one has, you know."

They were received by Marie, and taken to Miriam's sitting-room. They found her sitting quietly by the open window, reading a book. She was dressed in deep mourning.

As they went in, she rose to her feet and greeted them, with a gentle, patient dignity of bearing that impressed them both against their will.

"It is kind of you to call," she said, when her guests were seated.

"We wanted to say how sorry we were to hear of your . . ." Phillipa began. She meant to finish with the word "anxiety", but Miriam forestalled her.

"My terrible loss," she said. "My great and tragic loss. How kind of you both. I understand you are staying at Perros. That was where Giles said his boat is now, I think."

"No. We came back here yesterday."

Miriam's dark eyes flashed.

"In the river? Oh, then I shall see Giles again!" She clasped her hands in her lap to hide her agitation. "I was ill when he came before. Sick with fear and worry and uncertainty. I talked a lot of nonsense to him. I want him to see that I have recovered, now. I am more resigned. Poor Henry. He never told me what he meant to do. He was always so reserved. So withdrawn. I could have helped him, but he would never let me do so. He made up his mind alone, as always."

"What do you mean?" Phillipa asked.

The gentle voice wavered a little, but she went bravely on.

"I am sure now that my poor Henry has taken his own life. He was beginning to find things too much for him, you know. He was always ill. He could do less and less with his hands, and his heart was affected."

She repeated all she had told Inspector Renaud, only reversing the Paris specialist's verdict on Henry's heart. Also the detail was firmer now: there were added touches of observation. It all sounded most convincing.

"But you can't be certain," Phillipa protested. "His body has not been found. Or has it?"

Her voice was harsh, and her question most unsuitably abrupt. Miriam's eyes opened wide at such unexpected boorishness.

"No. He has not been found—yet. But I am sure. I feel it—here."

She pressed her hand against the black bodice of her dress. "I feel certain," she said. "Both that he is dead, and that he took his own life."

While the Marshalls sat looking at her, incapable of continuing this outrageous conversation, the door opened, and with exultant speed Giles and Susan came in, their faces glowing, radiant.

"Good morning, Miriam," Giles said, losing something of his exuberant manner in that sombre presence. "I'm sorry if this isn't the right moment to make an announcement, but I can't keep it back. Sue and I are going to be married."

Tony and Phillipa jumped up to kiss and congratulate the happy couple. But Miriam, making no sound, lay back in her chair, eyes closed, the colour draining slowly from her face.

CHAPTER XV

THERE WAS AN embarrassing silence. The four who stood round Miriam, watching her consciously prolonged recovery, were filled with a most uncomfortable guilt. Their English sense of fair play was outraged. They knew that Henry was alive, probably quite near at hand, and they were forced to withhold their knowledge. Away from Miriam, it had been easy to say she herself was the guilty one, and had deserved the situation in which she was now placed. But in her presence, watching her struggle for control, her white face more sharply beautiful in her real distress than it had ever been in the false roles she had played to them before, they forgot the would-be murderess, and saw only a suffering immature woman, alone among enemies and unwilling betrayers.

But not yet beaten. She rallied with surprising speed. As always, she recoiled furiously from reality, her imagination stimulated and fortified by the energy of her refusal. She ignored altogether the news of the engagement. She said politely to Giles, "I do hope your boat is all right now. They didn't take very long to mend it, did they?" Then she turned to Phillipa and Tony and began a trivial conversation about the limitations of the shops in Penguerrec. Giles turned abruptly and walked out of the room. As he shut the door he heard her say, "Susan dear, I have one or two things I want Francine to do for me. I've got a list somewhere. Don't go just yet."

He was both sick at heart and furious with Miriam for her implied insult. Also with himself for his own helplessness. He cursed himself for interfering at all. If he had not rushed off, looking for Henry, he would have had nothing to tell the police and could not have been forced into his present unwilling collaboration with them. He had discovered nothing Inspector Renaud had not found out for himself.

As he stood in the hall, hoping that Susan would find an excuse to join him, or that Pip and Tony, at any rate, would end their visit, Francine came through the door from the kitchen premises. As usual she was wearing an apron over her black dress, and wiped her hands on it when she saw him. He noticed that her cheeks were very pink, and she was slightly out of breath, as if she had been hurrying. Her first words confirmed this.

"I was afraid I might miss you," she said. "You have seen Madame?"

"For a few minutes, yes."

"Then she knows you are here again, with your yacht?"

"Yes. My friends called a little before I did."

She looked at him, steadily.

"She is very ill, monsieur."

This agreed with his own uneasy conclusion. But he did not want to discuss Miriam with the old woman.

"She is naturally very anxious and upset," he said, unwillingly.

"It is more than that. Look how she brought in the police with her hints that Mademoiselle had committed a dreadful crime. She is saying now that Monsieur Henri took his own life."

"Is she, indeed?"

"Yes, monsieur. But I think she does not really believe that. I think she has the intention of taking her own."

"Of committing suicide?" He was indignant. "Nonsense. It's the last thing she'd do."

Francine's eyes narrowed.

"Why do you say that, monsieur?"

"Because she is in love with herself, and always has been, and always will be! Because she spends her time inventing new parts for herself to play, in which she is the heroine. Painful parts, very often, but all false. So false that she has only to stop playing them for the whole thing to disappear. She would never do anything to cause herself actual pain. Certainly not *death*."

He stopped speaking, appalled at what he had said, but knowing it to be true.

"You are very bitter, monsieur. Very hard. I appeal to you

for the last time. Take her away from here before it is too late."

Stung beyond measure by Francine's blind persistence, Giles threw away his promise to the inspector.

"It is already too late," he said. "What you suggest is now impossible."

Francine stared at him without moving. Her dark eyes widened a little as he spoke, but the light in them was dulled almost at once. Her broad face, as always, held no expression. He wondered what she was thinking, hoping she had not really understood what he meant. He had not actually mentioned the police. Or Henry. Anyway, what business was it of Francine's? Why did her curiously formidable presence always have this effect on him? Of a hidden weight behind all her words; a persistent double meaning that was hidden from him. She was the housekeeper; the cook, too. An excellent cook. He realised that she must have come straight from the kitchen to intercept him in the hall. Those pink cheeks, that fishy smell about her. Yes, oysters. She must have been opening oysters for lunch. He noticed a small strip of bright green seaweed on the elbow of her dress as she lifted her hand to her hair. Fresh oysters straight from the hard. He had seen them there that morning, in baskets, with seaweed and sand clinging to them. He remembered, at once, that the village must know by now of Henry's return, and therefore Francine. Why, he might be already in the house. That must be why she was urging him again to save Miriam.

Francine tucked a stray hair into the bun at the back of her head.

"I have done my best," she said. "I have done all I can."

Susan came out of Miriam's room. She went towards Francine, but Giles caught her hand.

"Madame," he said, formally. "Mademoiselle and I are going to be married. Now do you understand?"

The old woman bowed stiffly.

"Felicitations, monsieur, mademoiselle," she said, and turned away. Susan pulled her hand free.

"Darling, I must go after her. If they'll let me I'll come down to the hard this afternoon. Watch out for me."

He kissed her swiftly, and she ran away after Francine as Tony and Phillipa came into the hall.

The three friends walked back down the main drive to the gates. Here they were stopped by the policeman on guard.

"I have a message for you from Inspector Renaud," he said. "The inspector says you and your friends must not be in the château or the grounds or the woods by the river after two o'clock this afternoon. Not on any pretext whatever. That is understood?"

"Perfectly," said Giles.

"Thank you, monsieur."

He stood aside. They all said goodbye to him politely and made their way back to *Shuna*.

It was a scorching day. They bathed from the yacht, and dried themselves afterwards in the sun.

Giles said, "Susan's going to try to get out later on. It looks a bit doubtful after what that chap at the gate told us. Unless of course Miriam makes a grand confession when she sees Henry."

"I don't see what follows from that," Tony said. "Unless Henry really has a case, and charges her."

"If the police have a case, they can charge her themselves—with attempted murder."

"I don't think she'd ever confess," said Phillipa. "I think she'll simply have a superlative attack of hysteria and they'll all feel terrible, as we did, every time, and then sorry for her. As we all do now, don't we? In spite of everything?"

The men would not agree, but in their hearts they knew that Phillipa was right.

"I'm going to take the dinghy and try fishing the mouth of the creek," said Giles. "I can watch out for Susan from there. The tide will be right down between two and three. You two coming?"

"No. I've some postcards to write up for the kids," Tony answered, guessing that Giles would prefer to be alone.

"And I want to clean the stove," said Phillipa. "I haven't done it properly since we started this trip, and it looks as if we are going to be travelling non-stop from now on."

So Giles exchanged his bathing trunks for a pair of shorts and rowed slowly about among the rocks and little bays near the opening of the creek. At times he drifted, his fishing line trailing behind him. He had one or two bites, but each time the fish, whatever it was, got away. He caught one or two heavy pieces of seaweed. He did not mind his lack of success at all, for his mind was not on the job. Gradually, however, the gentle rocking of the boat, and the sound of the water all round him, and the bright sun burning into his naked back and arms and glittering from the many-coloured rocks, drew out the barbed thoughts that had tortured the end of his morning, almost killing his fresh joy. He was at peace again, and thankful that he had been forbidden to visit the château. He rejoiced to think he need never see Miriam again. His uneasy, reluctant feeling of responsibility for her vanished at last.

It was slack water now, and the mud, drying in the sun, began to smell too strongly close in-shore. Giles took the sculls and rowed further out into the river.

Inspector Renaud arrived at the house early that afternoon. His plans had been carefully laid. He had had a little trouble with Henry when he had explained them soon after the latter landed at Penguerrec; but in the end he had prevailed. Henry was still a sick man; that was obvious. He had not been capable of much resistance, at two o'clock in the morning, after a tedious uncomfortable passage in the *Marie Antoine*, even though the sea had been smooth. Inspector Renaud had soon persuaded him to put himself entirely in the hands of the police. What they proposed to do was all directed to his own safety and full recovery. He had only to rest, and then appear before Miriam at a given moment. Rest and sleep, the Inspector said, and we will do the rest.

In the hall of the house Inspector Renaud sent Marie away and gave final instructions to his subordinate.

"You will stay here," he said. "I will interview Madame first in her boudoir. Then I will take her upstairs to her bedroom. The communicating door with Monsieur Davenport's room is unlocked, as it has always been. When we have passed through the hall and mounted the stairs, you will follow and take Monsieur into his own bedroom. He is now waiting in the housekeeper's room with Madame Francine. I will explain to Madame Davenport all that we have discovered about the drug. Then we fling open the communicating door, and he is there, dressed in his usual clothes. Understood?"

"Perfectly," answered the other.

Inspector Renaud knocked at the door of Miriam's sitting-room, and without waiting, opened it and went in.

She was once more sitting by the open window, alone, and as the door opened she turned her pale, lovely face towards it. She did not speak or get up, but she gave the inspector a sad little smile of welcome that went straight to his heart and even shook his resolution a little. He noted, with pleasure, that black became her: softened, somehow, the theatrical impact of her appearance and personality. Besides, he was accustomed to think of black as a correct and chic colour for women's clothes.

After greeting her, Renaud asked where Susan was at that moment.

"I don't know," Miriam answered. "We lunched together and then she went upstairs. Probably to her own room. She will want to see you before you go. To ask permission to go out. She is engaged to be married to Mr. Armitage."

"I know," said the inspector. "Mademoiselle will want to leave soon for England, then?"

"Very soon, I imagine."

There was a pause. This was not the way Renaud had intended the conversation to go. He did not know how to deal with this new, calm, relaxed pose Madame had adopted. It was not in character. For one heart-chilling moment he wondered if Henry had succumbed, either to his illness, or to some fresh devilish attack on her part. But no, he had provided guard enough. Henry had been watched from the moment of his arrival. He pulled himself together.

"Following my instructions," he said, in his most official manner, "I must report to you that I am far from satisfied with your explanations. With any of your explanations. You have told me too many lies. You have also concealed too much.

Those twenty-four hours in Paris after you left your hotel. You did not explain that before leaving you made a telephone call to a certain Paris number. That two hours later a man called to see you. We have traced this friend of yours, madame. This old friend. He lent you money, not for the first time. He understood from you that you were going to leave your husband on grounds of cruelty. He had heard this story very often before. You spent some of that day going round various travel agencies together, because you intended to leave France altogether. Nothing was settled, I understand. But the intention was plain."

"I was so worried. I felt I could not bear any more."

"I understand that, madame. But you were not worried about your husband. It was on your own account, wasn't it?"

She whispered, "Yes," all the calm self-possession gone.

"Now as to the special drug, we have additional information. You said you took and hid the prescription to prevent your husband taking too much. This obliged him to write for further supplies, so preventing him from taking any for a time. But we have proof that you, yourself, wrote for fresh supplies. The quantity found in your room is not a quarter of the amount you, personally, obtained. How do you explain this, madame?"

Miriam began to shake all over; her hands, her feet, her head quivered and shook. She tried twice to stand up, but sank back each time, helpless. At last she managed to say, "He must have forged my writing! He must have hidden it in my room and taken it, on purpose. Suicide! I know it was suicide!"

"This is a new idea. Why should he conceal his supplies in your room? Why not in his own?"

"To put the blame on me. To make it seem my fault."

"You had a simple remedy, madame. To destroy all of the drug, instead of keeping it. At any rate, I take it you locked the drawer where it was?"

"Yes. No. I don't—remember."

Inspector Renaud got up.

"Perhaps you will show me, madame. You suggest that your husband came into your room, when you were asleep, perhaps, and took out the drug he had concealed there on purpose. We will go to your room, and you will show me where exactly you hid these extra supplies, and where you think *he* could have hidden them. I admit that I find your theory very confusing."

Helped by the inspector, Miriam tottered to her feet, and half supported, half propelled, was got upstairs to her room.

Here Renaud let her sit down again, and with her usual extraordinary resilience she began to recover, and even to boast of her ingenuity in hiding the medicine.

"I kept the communicating door locked on my side," she said. "Always, except of course when he asked to come to my room. He could not get in that way, unless I was here."

"But he could get in, surely, from the passage, at any time?"

"I think he would not dare unless he knew I was asleep."

"And I think that is nonsense," Renaud told her, rudely. "Also it destroys your own idea that he hid the drug himself in your room. You cannot have it both ways, you know."

"You confuse me," she wailed. "I don't know what I am saying."

"You know the truth," said the inspector. "That is all we want to hear. Monsieur Davenport's symptoms before he disappeared point to the fact that he was poisoned by that drug. Did you administer the poison?"

"No! NO!"

"Do you still hold that he has committed suicide?"

"He must have done. I think he must have done. He would not have taken so much by accident."

"How do *you* know, madame, how much he took?"

"I don't. You are making me say things. I know nothing!"

"Then we will ask Monsieur Davenport, himself, madame. Perhaps *he* will tell us the truth."

Miriam leaped to her feet. As Henry came slowly into the room she screamed once, the high, panic-stricken scream of a rabbit in a snare. Then she had gone, plunging out of the room and down the stairs before any of the men could reach her. She rushed across the hall and into her sitting-room, banging the door behind her and locking it on the inside.

Susan heard the noise and came out on to the landing. Francine and the two maids ran from the kitchen. Inspector Renaud and his sergeant bounded down the stairs.

"In her room," cried Francine. "I heard the key turn in the lock."

The combined efforts of the men burst in the door. But the room was empty. The open window showed them which way she had gone.

Giles, not having caught a single fish worth keeping in two hours of that lazy sunny afternoon, was winding up his line before rowing back to *Shuna* when he heard Miriam calling to him from the bank above the landing-stage.

Or rather, calling *for* him. Looking round over his shoulder he saw her standing there, gazing wildly about her, vainly searching the river for the yacht she expected to see quite close, and which was not there. She did not notice, or did not recognise, the solitary fisherman in his little boat. She called and called, in urgent need, in terrified despair.

For a moment Giles hesitated. Clearly she did not see him; with the sun in her eyes, perhaps he was hidden. So much the better. He had had enough—more than enough—of her. It would do no good to either of them to meet again. There was no way any more to help her; nothing whatever he could do.

That moment of hesitation on his part, of blindness on hers, sealed her fate. If he had responded when she first called out she might have stayed where she was, waiting for him. But she caught sight of him just as he was picking up his oars to row away.

"Giles!" she screamed. "Don't go! Don't leave me, Giles! Take me with you! *You must take me with you!*"

Moving with desperate haste she flung herself forward, turned, seized the head of the top ladder and trod swiftly down the first rungs. There was a tearing, rending sound, and the whole ladder came away from the stage, with Miriam clinging to it.

To Giles, frozen with surprise and horror, the whole thing seemed to happen in slow motion. The ladder moved inexorably outwards and began to fall. Miriam's feet fell away from it, leaving her hanging by her hands alone. As her grip weakened she began to scream, her hands slipped from the rungs and she fell ten feet to the stage below. With the final jerk she gave it, the ladder's lower supports, long spikes dug into the mud, swivelled up out of it, and the whole heavy iron structure fell on her sprawled body. Her shrieks were cut off suddenly, her legs jerked convulsively twice, and were still.

Giles reached the end stage in a couple of minutes. It was the only one of the three afloat. As he clambered up the first ladder he heard her moaning, and knew that she was alive. But he had seen the great iron bar of the ladder strike her back, and he knew what he would find.

He came to her, and stooped, and with a great effort, straddling her body, lifted the thing away from her. Then he knelt, very gently moving her head to turn her bruised face a little, so that she could breathe more easily. She was quite conscious, still mad with fear. Her mouth opened to scream again, but no sound came. She clutched at him with a frenzied hand.

"Don't move. Lie still," he urged.

"I can't move," she whispered. "I can't move my legs."

"Don't try. Just lie still. I must get help."

"No one can help me now," she said, and closed her eyes. Weak tears flowed from them down her pale cheeks.

The police and Susan, the gardener and Francine, all appeared at the top of the bank while Giles was wondering if it was safe to leave her.

Renaud grasped the situation very quickly. He was not a Breton for nothing. A boat must bring her off, he saw at once. A stretcher, a boat, an ambulance at the hard. None of them at the top of the bank could reach the stage where she lay from the landward side until the tide was up again. They all hurried away to begin the rescue operations, and Giles sat down beside Miriam.

He took her hand and stroked it, praying for immediate death to forestall her further agony. The sun beat down on them. He had gone fishing without shirt or sweater. He had nothing to shield her with, or even to put under her head.

But she did not complain. Reality had been forced upon her

at last, in a most terrible form; not only her body had been shattered, but her belief in her own supremacy. She was dazed, and her wandering thoughts were not any longer on her present predicament.

"Henry," she murmured, presently. "Henry is alive."

"Yes," he answered.

"Did you know?"

He could not bring himself to acknowledge this. "Hush," he said. "Don't talk. It'll tire you."

"Henry has won," she whispered. "He has killed me. I knew that he wanted to kill me."

"Hush," he said, again, but for the first time he was ready to believe her. The ladder ought to have been mended. In any case the rope he had put on it should have held with only Miriam's weight. It could not have been mended, and where was the rope? Glancing over his shoulder he saw no sign of it on the fallen ladder, or the stage. So perhaps she was right; had been right all the time. She had been engaged in a grim duel, which she had lost.

Her hand stirred under his. She did not open her eyes, but began to speak again, in the new weak voice that hurt him more even than her terrible screams.

"I had to defend myself. It was not wicked to defend myself."

He had to answer this. "There were other ways. You could have left him. But you must not think of it all now. I understand."

"Do you? I wonder if you do." She opened her eyes, to fix his attention upon her. "I have always loved you, Giles. No, don't stop me. I have no strength to fight you now. I never loved Henry. But I was greedy. You were so poor, in those days. I was afraid of it. Henry seemed to be rich. There was the château. It sounded so wonderful. If only I had waited."

He was sickened by the meaning behind her cheap words. Again she had forgotten George, his own immediate successor; also the procession of later poor dupes that Henry had watched. The old Miriam was still alive, and even now, reviving. The moment of honesty was over.

. "No," he said. "No. This isn't the time. You mustn't say such things. Not now. Not after . . ."

"I have always loved you, Giles," she insisted, in the same weak, compelling whisper. "When I am better . . ."

"No," he said again, immeasurably shocked. "No. No."

He had to stop her lying tongue, because he knew she was finished, there was no possible recovery, and he could not endure that she should so profane her death.

CHAPTER XVI

IT TOOK TWO hours to get Miriam away from the landing-stage and back to her room at the château.

Giles stayed with her. He did what he could to comfort the slow minutes of waiting, and then, when a motor boat came off from the hard, bringing a stretcher and blankets, he showed the scared fishermen on board how to move her on to it, without bending or jarring her injured spine. By the time they got her to Penguerrec, an ambulance had arrived to take her on to a hospital, but she refused absolutely to go there. Giles argued with her, the ambulance men protested and explained, but all to no purpose.

"I will die in my own room," she kept repeating.

"But you may not die at all. You may be completely cured."

"My legs are paralysed. I shall never walk again."

Giles saw that reality had thrust upon her once more. His rôle was reversed. It was now he who pretended. But it was no good, in the end they had to give in to her. They had to, because she began to lift herself on her arms, threatening to drag herself from the stretcher and make an end there and then. So they drove her to the château, and carried her into the hall.

Inspector Renaud and the rest came crowding round her; Henry, Susan, Francine—even Marie and Lucette, peeping white-faced from the door leading to the kitchens.

Renaud was furious. Miriam had baulked him again. She had not made the expected confession, so he was no further with the case than before. This accident would undoubtedly rouse public sympathy on her behalf, perhaps with censure for himself. He tried to stamp out the difficulty.

"This woman is under arrest," he cried. "She is under my orders!"

Giles was shocked at such a callous claim, and doubted the truth of it. He was about to protest when Henry forestalled him.

"You cannot arrest her," he said. "She has committed no crime."

Renaud turned on him.

"She tried to murder you! You yourself have charged her with this crime."

"I charge her with no crime," said Henry, steadily. "I deny it, and shall deny it in any court you take it to."

"And if you die, monsieur, as you still may, as a result of the poisoning?"

"If I die, I shall no longer be concerned with the case."

Miriam, staring up from the stretcher, met her husband's eyes, and they exchanged a long, strange look, in which there was no hatred and no fear, only a sort of brooding speculation.

"If I die first," she asked, "will my murder come home to you, Henry?"

No one answered her. At a sign from the inspector the ambulance men stooped to lift her.

Giles said, "Has anyone sent for a doctor? She ought not to be moved off the stretcher until a doctor has seen her."

"I have telephoned for a specialist," Henry answered. "He will be here any time now. He was bringing a portable X-ray apparatus with him."

"Did you know, then, she would refuse to go to hospital?"

"Yes," he said, without bothering to explain his certainty.

Susan slipped her cold hand into Giles's. They moved back a little from the group round the stretcher.

"He wouldn't have let her go if she'd wanted to," she whispered. "It was the first thing he said."

"When?"

"Inspector Renaud told him she'd had an accident and he was sending her to hospital. Henry said he wouldn't let her go. Just like that."

"How very odd."

"I know. Horrible. It's all horrible, isn't it? Not just the accident. Them."

He pressed her hand and let it go. Horrible was indeed the word for this tangling of a slippery web of malice and greed and revenge and hatred. They were like two snakes engaged in a slow battle to the death, each with jaws fixed in the other's flesh, holding and waiting.

The ambulance men were discussing the situation with Inspector Renaud. They had lowered the stretcher again to the floor.

"We will leave the stretcher if you will undertake to return it. But we must take the blankets, except of course the one folded under her."

"Shall I bring blankets?" asked Francine, who had been standing all the time with folded hands waiting for orders.

"Can't we get her up to her room?" Giles burst out, sickened by all this discussion. "Let them take the top blankets, now. I know where there's a rug to use instead."

He strode to the cupboard in the hall where he and his friends had hung their wet oilskins when they had come to stay in the house. He remembered clearly seeing a pile of rugs there on the floor at one side. He flung the door open.

There were the rugs, as he expected. But there also, hanging from the pegs, were Henry's duffle coat, his fisherman's jersey, the blue blouse he wore as an onion man, the jeans, and below, thrown in, it seemed, in a hurry, his fisherman's rubber boots, still wet, covered with fresh mud and weed, and stinking of it, too, in that confined space.

Giles snatched up two rugs and went back to the group round Miriam. They exchanged the rugs for the blankets, the men lifted the stretcher, and the sad little procession went up the stairs, Susan leading and Renaud bringing up the rear. He was determined to watch his "prisoner", as he still regarded her, until the specialist arrived and he knew something definite of her condition and probable fate.

When Miriam was out of hearing, Giles turned to Henry.

"Your boots," he said, with a biting emphasis on every word. 'Don't you think you had better clean the mud—the river mud —off them, while it is still wet? It might be more difficult when it dries on."

Henry stared at him. Francine stared at Henry, alarm in her dark eyes. The Englishman's voice held a menacing note. Neither of them spoke.

"I'm going now," Giles said. "Tell Susan to come down to the hard as soon as she can get away. I'll be waiting for her. I shan't come back here—ever. I don't want to see this place again, or you, or Miriam. You needn't be afraid I'll tell anyone what I now know. You and Miriam appear to be quits, if that is the right word. And there couldn't be a worse punishment for either of you than what seems to be coming to you both. I only hope to God I haven't, unintentionally, speeded things up. But I don't see how I could have prevented it."

He went through the silence to the door, and out into the sunlight, leaving it open behind him.

Francine sighed, smoothed her black skirt with both hands, and moving quietly to the staircase, began to mount.

But Henry darted to the hall cupboard and dragged open the door. He looked at the boots, turned them over with his foot, and then left them there, locking the cupboard door, and taking away the key. He stumbled into the library, and sinking down in the chair by his desk laid his head on his arms, sobbing his heart out in despair, for his weakness and hesitation, and the failure of all he had ever meant to achieve.

Giles strode off down the drive towards the main gates. But when he was out of sight of the house, he stopped. He remembered that his dinghy was still tied up to the landing-stage. It would be much quicker and better in every way to take it from there himself. It meant climbing down the first steep drop of the bank, from the top part of the stage, but by now the tide would be up to the next part of it. If he could not get down the bank at that spot, he might be able to scramble down further along and get into the water and swim back. He decided to do this.

The path through the woods was quite deserted. So was the landing-stage when he reached it. Evidently Inspector Renaud was not interested in the cause of Miriam's fall.

Giles stood on the top stage where the ladder had been. Two things were immediately obvious. First, the ladder had clearly not been mended after the original mishap. The broken iron had not been replaced, and the fractured end was rusty now from exposure to the salt air over the last few days. Secondly the rope he had put on himself, and which he had looked for on the stage below, was not up here either. It had been taken away.

It was easy to see what had happened. In her haste and guilty terror Miriam had flung herself on to the ladder without looking to see if it had been mended. If she thought of it at all, the absence of the rope probably led her to imagine repairs had been made. In any case there was nothing to remind her of the former damage.

Giles knelt down and looked over the edge of the bank. The ladder was still lying on the stage. He saw how it must have bent outwards under her weight, held for a time by its feet, planted firmly in the mud at the foot of the bank. Looking down at the ladder, he saw that the long spikes were indeed slightly bent. But only slightly. They should have bent more. They might even have broken off short. But this had not happened.

He moved along the bank to a place where rocks grew out of the mud, and scrambled down. Moving slowly from one firm spot to another, he made his way to the landing-stage. At times he was nearly up to his knees in the mud, which bubbled and stank as he plunged through it. But he held on and presently was standing below the drop, with the second stage lying on the mud only a few feet away.

And now he saw, to his great annoyance, that his recent flounderings had been quite unnecessary. A distinct track, made of steps cut in the mud, sloped up at an angle with the bank, to the firm ground beyond tide level. He had not seen them from above, because the bank overhung the spot. He had not noticed them while he was waiting on the stage with Miriam; his attention then had been all for her.

He was certain of one thing. On none of the other occasions when he and his friends had used the landing-stage had any of them seen steps in the bank. These had been made recently, and made with a purpose. To dig out the base of the ladder, and make quite certain it would fall the next time it was used.

Giles had suspected something of the sort when he found Henry's boots in the cupboard. Now he knew, and he felt suddenly very tired. He had meant what he said to Henry. It was up to Inspector Renaud; and the latter, in his pursuit of

L

Miriam, was going to miss the proof of her intended murder. The rising tide would carry away the temporary steps and fill in the dug-out holes at the foot of the bank. Let it rest. The guilt was shared; the punishment, too. Proof was too late; it had become irrelevant.

Giles went slowly along the two stages to his dinghy. Before getting into it he sat down to wash the mud off his legs and canvas shoes. Then, moving stiffly, feeling utterly worn out, he untied the little boat, climbed in, and pulled back, against the flood, to the haven and understanding of *Shuna*.

Tony and Phillipa did not ask many questions. They saw the state he was in. Tony got him a drink at once; told him briefly that they had gathered more or less what was happening.

"We were stuck," said Phillipa, "because you had the dinghy."

"I know."

"Was she—very badly hurt?"

"I'm afraid so."

They waited for him to go on, if he would. Instead, he said presently, "Susan. I asked Henry to tell her to come down to the hard when she could. I'll have to go off and wait for her."

"You stay where you are," Tony ordered. "I'll pick her up. I need some exercise."

Giles was too weary to argue. He finished his drink, went below, and stretched himself on his bunk. After a little while, being now out of the sun, he began to shiver, and realised that he still wore only the cotton shorts he had put on to go fishing. He found his shirt and a sweater and pulled them over his head. By this time he was too restless to lie down again, so he rejoined Phillipa on deck.

"I don't call that much of a rest," she said. "But never mind. Susan's come. Just arrived. With luggage."

"*Luggage?*"

He stared towards the shore. Susan was there, right enough. He could see her tall, slim figure, leaning against the sea wall. She had on a white shirt and black slacks. There were two suitcases at her feet. Her intention was perfectly clear. She had left the château and meant to travel on *Shuna*.

"Bless her," he said aloud.

Phillipa knew what he meant. There was no place now for Susan at the house, so she was coming to Giles, quite naturally and simply, for help and protection, and because she loved him. It was the kind of love he needed and deserved. She, too, blessed Susan in her heart.

Tony was back in a very short time. Giles helped Susan on board and followed her down to the cabin with her suitcases.

"They told me to go," she said. "I couldn't be any help. So can I go with you?"

He drew her into his arms, looking deep into the clear amber eyes.

"Always," he said. "Always and everywhere."

When they joined the others again on deck Susan explained what had been happening at the château after Giles left. The local doctor had arrived, almost at once, with a surgeon from the nearest orthopaedic hospital. They both urged Miriam to go away for treatment, but again she refused to be moved. Another specialist was called from Paris.

"I think she's right to stay," said Susan. "Her legs are paralysed. They can't do anything for her."

"If they set her back properly she might get some recovery. It could be just a concussion of her spinal cord, not a complete break."

"Do you really think so? How do you know?"

"I knew a chap once that had a car accident where the same sort of thing happened." But he remembered the iron ladder striking that sprawling defenceless back; the convulsive jerks; the flaccid limbs he had helped to lift on to the stretcher. No, he did not really think she would recover.

"What did Henry say? Didn't he change his mind, after that, and insist on her going?"

"He's in bed, himself. He collapsed in the library after we took her upstairs. Francine found him there. They had to carry him up, too."

"Pretty grim for you, altogether," said Tony. "Did the inspector tell you to go?"

"The doctors. They'd been talking to him. They said there was no place for me now in the house. Nurses were on their way. And of course Francine was there to run the place as usual."

After a pause Giles said, "It's unbelievable, really. This morning, all peaceful, even if quite artificial. I mean Miriam's act about Henry's suicide. I didn't believe a word of it. But I didn't expect such a sequel."

"No." Susan's face was full of pain. "No. She was so sure of herself at lunch. She thought she'd got everybody taped, even the inspector. I think she really believed Henry's body would turn up in the river and show he had died of drowning, and they wouldn't look for any other cause. She ate a really big lunch, for her."

"Oysters and all?" asked Giles.

"Oysters?" Susan was astonished.

"Didn't you have oysters?"

"We didn't have fish at all. We had a wonderful sort of Breton hash, only it has a much grander name than that."

"Giles," interrupted Phillipa. "When are we leaving? Do you want us to have dinner now?"

"Yes. We'd better."

"You can't guess what we're having," she said, as she turned on the companion-ladder.

"Oysters," they all cried in chorus.

CHAPTER XVII

THE TWO MEN prepared *Shuna* for sailing, while Phillipa helped Susan to stow her things below in one of the lockers. The suit-cases were disposed of in the forepeak, wedged firmly with spare coils of rope.

It was dark when *Shuna* left the river, but clear, as it had been the night before. The buoys in the channel winked bright-ly, La Corne lighthouse sent its beam flashing round over the rocks and the water between. Giles motored to save time, for the channel often changed direction, and he did not want to beat. But when he was clear of the in-shore marks he put up his sails and switched off the engine, and *Shuna* bounded on towards the open sea.

They had decided already, weather permitting, to go straight back to the Solent. Their holiday was nearly over, and none of them felt like staying on the French coast any longer.

"We've a fair breeze," Giles explained to Susan, as the land dropped away behind them. "We'll make up to the Casquets. We've still got a couple of days in hand. We can always go into Bray in Alderney if we change our minds. But personally I feel like getting home. How about you?"

"I feel like being sick," said Susan, faintly, and was so.

She spent most of that night on deck, secretly wishing she had not chosen to travel this way, even for Giles's sake. The others came up to take the helm at regular intervals, spending their time off watch quietly sleeping below. They made her share their frequent drinks of cocoa, which she promptly re-turned. At first light, quite exhausted, Susan at last gave in and crept down to a bunk, not caring any longer that the movement in the cabin was worse than on deck. To her enormous surprise she fell asleep at once, and when she woke it was seven in the morning, and she crawled back on deck and welcomed hot coffee and scrambled eggs, and kept it all down.

Giles pointed ahead.

"The Casquets," he said.

"Where?"

"Little white spike dead ahead."

She saw the lighthouse far off, with the spray breaking on the rocks below.

"Want a rest? Shall we go into Bray?"

"No. Let's go on. I don't want to start at the beginning again."

"Good girl. That's the spirit."

So they went on towards England, the westerly wind steady behind them. It died off during the afternoon, however, and left them at nightfall drifting on the fringe of the steamer lanes, ten miles out from the English coast. They were in no hurry now, so there was no point in motoring, unless they had to take action to avoid being run down. Just after midnight a very gentle air came up in the south, and they crept forward towards Poole Bay. By dawn the cliffs at the Needles stood out of a light mist in front of them, with the coast line of the Island fading away towards St. Catherine's Point.

Susan was thrilled, and said so.

"I know," Giles answered her. "There's nothing to compare with making a home landfall at dawn. Except picking up foreign lights in the middle of the night."

The others came into the cockpit to have a look at England and then Phillipa went below again to get breakfast. Susan was entrusted with the tiller for the first time, while Giles and Tony set the spinnaker to increase their speed.

"It steadies the roll, too," Giles explained to Susan. But she laughed. She had her sea legs by now, and when the bacon and eggs came up from below, she ate heartily. The others congratulated her.

"It seems simply ages since we left Penguerrec," she said. "Weeks. Months. Not only yesterday."

"The day before yesterday," Giles corrected her.

"Yes. Of course. I've lost count."

"One does," agreed Phillipa.

"I don't want to talk about it if you'd rather not," Susan went on, looking at Giles. "But I keep going over it all in my mind. That last day, I mean. And wondering what really happened."

"I know," he answered, in a low voice. "So do I."

"Why did the ladder fall?"

"Because it had not been mended, and my rope had been taken off and whoever did that dug out the feet of the ladder as well, to loosen the whole contraption."

"Could it have been Henry?"

"Not only could, but was. I found his boots in the cupboard in the hall, wet, with river mud all over them."

"But I thought the police had hold of him from the time he landed," Phillipa said, coming up the companion-way with the coffee pot in her hand. "Do you two want to stay out here or go below?"

The early sun, breaking out of the mist, touched Susan's hair, making the gold shine as it had in the Tréguier river.

"Here," said Giles.

"It's a pretty grim thought," said Tony, "that Henry was in the house, somewhere, without Miriam knowing. Francine must have seen him, even if the maids didn't. Someone would have to let him in."

"Why not Henry, himself?"

"Yes. I suppose he had his own keys. Anyway, the inspector must have been with him."

"I don't think they'd tell Francine," Susan argued. "She always seemed to be on Miriam's side."

"In a way," said Phillipa, thoughtfully. "She tackled me once about Miriam and Giles. I know, I didn't tell you at the time, Giles. It was so embarrassing. She said Miriam had kept your photograph. Actually she showed me a photograph of you both; one of those double frames. Later on, she told me Miriam had other photographs of men friends. I couldn't stop her, though she must have seen I didn't want to hear gossip. I think Francine knew everything that went on. I'm sure she'd know Henry had come back."

"Of course she would," said Giles. "But she didn't know more about Miriam than Henry himself did. He knew all about those scandals. He told me so in Southampton."

"The grocer's wife hinted at them, too. It must have been common knowledge."

"Do you mean," Susan asked, "that Francine was not a hundred per cent for Miriam? That she was deliberately blackening her character?"

"It looks a bit like it, now, don't you think?"

"Probably she was just trying to build up a very good case for getting Miriam to leave Henry, before he took really drastic action," Tony suggested.

"Miriam would never have gone," said Susan. "She was enjoying it all. She loved the feel of being martyred. I know she did."

"She'd have gone if I'd taken her," said Giles, giving voice to the thought in all their minds. "But Susan put a stopper on that, thank God."

He stretched out a hand to her knee, and she covered it with her own, while their eyes met, and stayed.

"I don't see why it shouldn't have been those fishermen in the village," Tony began again. "Responsible for all the odd things that happened, I mean. The hole into the tunnel and the notice board moved, and the broken ladder. I think as soon as it got about, via the maids and Francine, that the English visitors knew Madame, they foresaw another possible scandal, an outsize one at that, and set about driving us away, with their old Resistance techniques. Us. Not Miriam."

"I wonder."

"It fits all right. We had this out before. We were the strangers who wouldn't know where the secret tunnel was, or the quicksands. And who used the landing-stage. Besides, there was *Shuna*'s accident. You can't argue that was meant for Miriam by Henry or for Henry by Miriam. Incidentally we seem to have forgotten she tried to murder him."

"I haven't forgotten," said Giles.

"Nor I," said Susan, with a shiver.

"Well then. Look at it from the Penguerrec people's point of view. Their action against the yacht was successful. We left at once. But after a few days we came back, though we anchored at the harbour. They were not to know we meant to stay there, and not use the landing-stage. Perhaps Henry gave orders, after all, before he left, for the ladder to be mended. I think it's more likely he forgot, because he left himself that evening, didn't he?"

"So the village men arranged to wreck the ladder even more thoroughly than before?"

"No. I think it was a genuine accident the first time. Henry couldn't have put on the act he did, if he'd expected it. He'd have shown excessive concern to cover his guilt, not excessive reserve and every symptom of thinking it was meant for him."

"Oh, I don't know," said Phillipa. "If the new idea of Henry being a murderer is to hold water, you'll have to credit him with being a marvellous actor. Personally I can't believe it."

Giles had been considering Tony's theory.

"I'm sorry, old boy," he said, presently. "But your idea won't work. The Penguerrec types couldn't have laid that trap for *us*, during the night Henry came back."

"Why not?"

"For one thing, I was awake, on and off, most of it. I heard *Marie Antoine*'s engines start up, and the men calling to one another. That's why I went on deck. And I'm certain no boat went up the river to the stage. I'd have heard it, and gone up to see."

"You said you found steps in the bank. Doesn't that mean the job was done from the landward end?"

"With the gendarmerie as keen as they were on the job? I very much doubt it. Anyway, the point is it couldn't have happened in the night?"

"Why not?"

"The tide, fathead. Those steps in the bank, when I saw them, were fresh cut. At low water, of course. A couple of hours before. When the inspector's little game was on. When the police check in the grounds had been called off. When I was in the creek, fishing, and you two were having your siesta, or anyway, not looking up the river towards the stage. When the job could have been done by land. If the steps had been made at the previous low water, in the night, they'd have been blotted out, or partly so, at any rate."

"I'm a clot," said Tony. "Wash that out."

"The trap was laid at midday, or just after," Giles went on. "It must have been. I don't know where Henry spent the rest of the night, after he landed, but I think it must have been at the house. Renaud didn't want anyone in the village to see him, to avoid the possibility of them telling Miriam."

"But if he was at the house, as we said before, someone there must have known, even if only Francine. And I thought we decided she was on Miriam's side."

"You did," said Giles. "I didn't."

"Oh." Phillipa was excited. "Of course. I did hear that she brought him up. Francine, I mean. So perhaps she knew what he was up to, and was out to camouflage it."

"She was certainly very upset when he disappeared. But apart from that, the whole thing seems to me perfectly clear, on the very direct evidence of Henry's boots, mud-stained, and his fisherman's clothes, thrown into that hall cupboard."

"Pretty damning," agreed Tony.

"But they weren't hidden," cried Susan. "Were they really just chucked in anyhow?"

"No. Actually, the clothes were hanging on the pegs."

"It's damning, all the same," said Tony.

"But he hadn't tried to hide them," Susan insisted. "If he did it, as he may have, why didn't he hide the evidence?"

"Probably thought it wouldn't matter. Or couldn't be proved. Actually, I suppose it can't be. He landed at the low tide in the night, when the hard is muddy, too. That would be his defence. And you can't break it. But I looked back as I left the house and *I* saw him look at the boots, after I'd pointed them out to him, and *I* saw him shut the cupboard door and lock it and go away into the library. I saw his face. I know."

"How horrible!"

"I still don't see how he knew Miriam would go to the stage. Why should she? We weren't using it. *Shuna* was a long way off."

"She didn't know that. She knew we were back, when we called, and I expect she thought we had the boat in the same placc as before. Henry knew the inspector was going to arrange the confrontation. Naturally, he decided that the first thing the guilty Miriam would think of would be escape. Anywhere—by any means—to avoid immediate arrest. And therefore she would run to us—or rather, me. He knew her very well. He was right. She came straight down to the river. I saw her at the top section of the stage, looking wildly about and calling for me. And then . . .''

"Don't," said Susan, gently, wrung by the pain in his face. "It was not your fault. Nothing was your fault. She had no right to make such demands on people. No one has."

There was a long silence in the cockpit. Phillipa took the cold remains of breakfast below, and Susan followed her to help wash up. Giles handed the tiller to Tony and went forward himself, to sit down on the forehatch and watch the beautiful shape of the spinnaker bellying out above him, drawing *Shuna* along, while the little waves hissed under her bows.

They passed the Bridge buoy at the Needles at nine, the stream running now in their favour. It carried them past the narrows at Hurst, and on into the Solent.

"Are you going into Yarmouth?" Tony asked.

"No. Why?"

"I just wondered if you wanted to clear customs there."

"They can come to me on my own mooring. I'd rather go straight in."

So they sailed on up the Solent and turned into the Beaulieu river, where Giles had a mooring near Bucklers Hard. They flew their yellow flag from the entrance of the river, and after they had picked up the mooring and taken down the sails and tidied the decks, they sat down to wait.

"I ought to ring up my aunt," Susan said. "I'll have to go and stay with her for a week or two, as I'm back so early. I hope she can have me."

"Why don't you come to us?" said Phillipa.

"That's terribly sweet of you, but I think I'd better go to Aunt Mary if she can have me. She lives almost next door to us, so that would be very convenient for getting the house open again. She was expecting me, anyway, at the end of the month."

"You can't go ashore before we're cleared," Giles told her.

"At least, you're not supposed to, and they don't like it in this country if yachts break too many of the rules."

"You didn't have to do anything about customs in Brittany, did you?"

"There was a type who asked me for particulars the morning after we got to Penguerrec," Giles answered. "No forms or that sort of thing. They can't be bothered. But they're very hot on it, in England."

In about an hour the customs' launch came round from Southampton, having been warned by the harbour-master at Bucklers Hard. The crew of *Shuna* had so little to declare that the customs' officers became quite suspicious. Giles explained that they had been visiting friends abroad, where there had been sudden illness, which prevented them shopping in the last days before sailing home. This went down reasonably well, and the usual formalities were finished in a friendly spirit.

The whole party then went ashore. Both the Marshalls and Giles had cars, wrapped up in plastic covers, standing in the car park above the hard. Tony and Phillipa went ahead to get theirs uncovered, but Giles and Susan turned off into the Master Builders' Hotel to find a telephone.

When Susan had arranged to go to her Aunt Mary, Giles said, "I want to ring up Penguerrec. Have you got the number, by any chance?"

"Yes, I have. I was thinking of that, too. It's nearly two days since it happened, isn't it?"

They put the call in hand, and then ordered drinks and a table for lunch.

"No more cooking on board, Pip," Giles told her, when the Marshalls joined them.

"Nice of you," she answered.

"I'm driving Sue home," he went on. "Newbury, was it?"

She laughed.

"You heard me say the exchange, didn't you? You don't miss anything. Yes, near Newbury."

The call from Brittany came through about twenty minutes later. Giles went away to take it. When he came back, he sat down slowly, looking round at them in turn. Susan slipped her hand into his.

"Francine answered," he said. "The doctors say Miriam's spinal cord has been crushed, and there will be no recovery, though she may live for some time, even years. Henry is worse. He is in bed again, with severe shock and a return of his symptoms of poisoning. His condition is dangerous."

There was a long silence.

"So they may both die, after all," said Tony, presently. "It's a pretty nasty thought, them lying there, next door to each other, hating each other's guts, and waiting to see who's going to be out first."

"Don't," said Phillipa.

"Recurrence of poisoning," said Giles, heavily. "If that's true, he must have taken it himself, this time. Miriam couldn't be responsible, again."

"Perhaps she never was," said Susan. "Perhaps she was right about suicide."

"Do you really think that?" he asked her.

"Not before. No. But perhaps now—after Miriam's accident. If it *was* an accident, and he never did anything at all to harm her. Or it could be remorse, I suppose."

"It was no accident," said Giles. "Let's accept that once and for all. Henry meant to kill her, and it looks as if he succeeded."

"An empty success," said Phillipa, "if he happens to die first."

Susan shuddered.

"Was there anything we could have done to prevent it?" she asked. "Anything we might have said—to either of them?"

"No," Giles answered. "Nothing would have made any difference in the end. It must all have started years ago. Long before any of us came on the scene, thank God."

He did not yet know how right he was in this.

CHAPTER XVIII

MIRIAM DIED THREE months later. Henry recovered.

Only Susan, of Henry's English relations, went to the funeral. This was because the Brockley parents had prolonged their stay in the West Indies as soon as they heard of her engagement. In fact, they were thinking of settling there permanently, they wrote, since life was easier, with domestic help available, and the climate very pleasant. They were staying on to explore the possibilities, but would, of course, come back before Christmas to arrange for the wedding.

Susan showed the letter to Giles, who reflected that as his future in-laws thought only of themselves, he would miss very little if they made a new home out of England. The letter showed no interest in Susan's plans, and made only one reference to himself.

When Miriam died, the Brockleys were at sea, coming back to England. So Susan went alone to the funeral, refusing Giles's offer to go with her.

"I'll be all right, darling. I'm only staying one night. It seems so far away now; the accident, and what we thought must have happened..You don't really want to come, do you?"

"I should hate it. And so, I'm sure, would Henry. I only suggested it in case you had the wind up."

"What about? Henry? I decided long ago that we shall never know what really happened."

So Susan went to Brittany alone. She arrived at the château in the morning and the funeral took place at noon, in Tréguier, not Penguerrec. Miriam, it appeared, had been converted to the Catholic faith during her last illness. She was buried in a Catholic churchyard. Henry, Susan, and Francine were the only mourners present at the ceremony. Afterwards they drove back to the house.

There was no gathering of friends and relatives, no distressing funeral feast, for which Susan was profoundly grateful.

Henry took her to the library, where a cheerful fire was burning, and Francine brought them lunch; hot soup, and cold chicken with salad. The house was very quiet. Too quiet.

"Marie and Lucette did not come—with us," Susan began, following this thought.

"They are not here any longer," Henry answered. "Now that the nurses have gone, it was not necessary to keep them."

"Can Francine manage alone, in this big house?"

He hesitated, seemed about to break into some confidence, but changed his mind, and stared at the fire instead, aimlessly stirring his soup.

"Had Miriam no—parents—or anyone of her own—living?" she asked.

He looked up at her; dull eyes in an expressionless face.

"It was her last wish that none of them should know of her death until it was all over. She has written letters to them. She showed them to me. I was to send them today."

He bent his head, to hide his face from Susan.

"She tells them that her death was a just punishment," he said, very low. "A just punishment for her life. She became very religious towards the end. I think it helped her. There is nothing specific in the letters."

Susan felt a wave of disgust sweep over her. Miriam's conduct showed little or no change in her character. The same heightened emotion, the same hankering after melodrama. This first reaction of Susan's was followed by a chill of fear. Such words from a proved murderer. She choked, and quickly swallowed another mouthful of soup to cover it. When she looked up she saw Henry's cold eyes on her.

They continued the meal. Susan wanted to ask about Miriam's last days, but she could not bring herself to break into Henry's strange control. His sole confidence had been too disconcerting. After that, anything she might ask would sound like morbid curiosity.

A watery November sun touched the bare branches of the trees outside the window.

"I think I will go for a walk to the village," she said. "I want to send a telegram to my aunt."

"You can send it over the telephone from here."

"I know. But—I would like a walk. And you would rather be alone, Henry. Wouldn't you?"

He looked quickly at her and away again. In that brief moment she saw his unappeasable grief laid bare, and at the same time was deeply convinced of his guilt.

She took up the tray and carried it to the kitchen. Francine was sitting up to the kitchen table, eating heartily, the dishes spread in a semi-circle round her plate, the morning's newspaper propped up against them.

She did not get up when Susan came in, but nodded her thanks, and went on with her meal.

"I shall return tonight," Susan began, suddenly making up her mind. "Monsieur Henri does not want me here. I can do nothing to comfort him."

"It will pass," said Francine, woodenly. "He is still very frail."

"But surely—I thought he had quite recovered?"

"From poisoning, yes. But there is always his back. That does not improve. And then there is the deep impression on his mind of the attempt on his life. It is not funny, mademoiselle, to be attacked with poison. And by your wife."

She said this in a hard, coarse way that shocked Susan profoundly. The girl went out of the kitchen without answering, put on her coat, tied a scarf round her head, and went out.

The drive was thick with fallen leaves, pressed into two muddy ruts where car-wheels had passed in and out. The low sun touched the trunks of the trees here and there with streaks of gold, but the air was dank and chill. Susan gave a sigh of relief as she came out on to the road. The fields were brown from the plough, with seagulls scattered over them searching for food. The village lay in the sun. The boats rocked gently in the harbour.

Susan rang up the airport at St. Malo and managed to change her flight. Then she sent off a telegram to her aunt, telling her she was coming back that evening. As she left the post office she saw the grocer's wife, standing at the door of her shop. The woman spoke to her in a friendly voice and asked her to come in and warm herself by the fire.

"I am quite alone," she said, laughing. "My husband and my daughter have gone to the town. And besides," she added, when they were in the warm room behind the shop. "I am curious to hear about poor Madame Davenport's funeral. How she suffered! It was unbelievable!"

And now Susan was thankful for Henry's reticence, if what the grocer's wife said was true. She did not understand all the detail, but gathered enough from the frank Gallic description to realise what Miriam's last weeks had meant, in pain and degradation.

"Whatever her sins, and they were great," said the grocer's wife, piously, enjoying herself to the full, "she made a good end. Our curé was with her to the last."

"She became a Catholic, didn't she?"

"She was a devout convert. Very sincere. A fortunate thing, for she could repent and gain absolution, and that would not have been possible if she had remained a heretic."

"I see," said Susan, happy to think that Miriam had achieved something, in her own eyes at least, to offset all she had lost.

"Will you be here long?" asked the grocer's wife, politely.

"No. I am going back tonight. I—they don't need me. My cousin is very unhappy, but I can do nothing to help him."

The other nodded.

"I can understand that. Besides, he is well looked after. He has Madame."

"Francine? Yes. But the two girls have left, I hear."

The grocer's wife gave her a strange look.

"They were both of the—what shall I call it—the other faction."

"I don't understand."

"No, mademoiselle, you were not in France in the war. You English did not suffer occupation. I am not bitter myself, you understand? In Paris we were more philosophical. But here, there was a strong maquis. Madame was at the château all the time the Germans were there. She and her friends in the village killed five of them and stole many of their secrets. Hostages

M

were taken from the village and shot, in revenge, but the maquis was not broken, and was not betrayed. They are tough, the Bretons!"

"They are, indeed!"

"But no one forgets the hostages; certainly not their families. And Madame Francine was never suspected by the Germans, though everyone here knew she was at the head of the maquis. She is formidable, amazing!"

"Yes."

Susan got up to go. She thought the conversation had strayed too far from Henry and Miriam. There were enough painful memories at the château already, without adding to them Francine's lurid war-time past.

"My husband was in the Resistance," said the grocer's wife, as they shook hands in the shop. "That is why I have heard so much about Monsieur Henri and the fishermen."

"Thank you. You have been very kind," Susan told her.

She walked slowly back to the house, but when she was going up the drive she turned off down the path to the creek. It was in the shelter of the trees, at the edge of the bank above the sand, that Giles had asked her to marry him. She would never again come with him to this place, so she wanted to see it once more and to sit down on the fallen tree trunk and think over all the strange events of that tragic fortnight in August.

But she did not sit down. In the wood she had been able to imagine those days of summer and to bring back the first joy of her love. But not here. The tide was out. The flat stretch of sand, running down to foetid mud, rubbish-strewn, repelled her. Over the ruffled, iron-grey waters of the creek a biting wind from the east withered her romantic desires. She stood for a few seconds only, gazing on a scene of desolation unredeemed by any grandeur. The creek, like the house above, was a backwater, a repository of cast-off treasures, a harbour of imprisoned, festering, derelict hopes.

The place was quite deserted. She saw no footprints above the tide mark, no signs that anyone had come there since the equinoctial gales had washed away all the summer's litter and left a fringe of wrack close to where she was standing. As she began to turn away, she saw that Henry's notice board, the danger sign, had also gone. Not moved, this time; not fallen down and left on the ground; but taken away altogether.

She walked back towards the house, feeling more depressed than ever. But when she reached it she did not go in. Instead she walked on, finding her way round the outside of the walled garden to the path through the woods and the clearing with the view.

She found what she expected. The seat, Miriam's seat, had gone, too. The place where it had stood, over the cover to the hidden passage, was bare, though the grass had begun to spread over it. She moved away the damp soil at the edge with her foot, exposing a layer of cement that now held the cover in place. It would never be moved again.

Susan left the clearing. She walked on down the hill towards the river. As she came out of the trees she could not help giving a low cry of distress and astonishment. The whole scene immediately before her eyes was changed. The path no longer led to the landing-stage. It led nowhere. The whole stage had gone, and with it the launch, and the dinghy. The place where they had been was unrecognisable, for the bank had been cut back almost to where she stood. She looked down a muddy slope to the river below. It was some comfort to lift her eyes into the distance, and see the fishing boats at Penguerrec just as they had always been, and beyond to the west the dark hill at Pen Paluch.

She remembered that she had not yet told Henry she was flying back to England at once. She looked at her watch. If she did not hurry she would miss her train to St. Malo. Shaken at last from her deep sense of disillusion, she climbed the hill again to the house.

Henry listened to her halting explanation in silence, but seemed pleased with her decision. He carried her suitcase to the taxi himself and leaned into it when she was settled, to take her hand and thank her for coming.

"You *are* better, Henry, aren't you?" Susan asked, suddenly anxious, for his face looked so very pale and drawn in the half-light of the cab.

"If I could work," he answered, in a low voice. "If I could only work . . . I might begin to forget. At least, for part of the time."

"Forget what she did to you? Henry, I don't think she meant it. She was acting out one of her fantasies. She didn't really know what she was doing. She was so dreadfully afraid."

"Yes," he answered. "She was afraid. And her fear was justified. That is why I shall never forget, and never forgive myself. Day and night I shall never be able to stop thinking of it— her fear—and her death."

He must have felt Susan's hand shrink in his, for his face changed at once, taking on its usual blank politeness. He drew back and spoke to the taxi driver, then said through the window, "Remember me to my aunt and uncle," and turned away.

He was back in the house and closed the door before the taxi began to move.

Susan's parents arrived back in England the day after she returned from Brittany. She had begun to get the house ready a week before Miriam's death, so the interruption caused by this event did not mean any confusion. She had everything in order and ready for them; which, as usual, they took for granted.

"The garden is looking very neglected," Mrs. Brockley said, a few hours after her arrival.

"Well, yes. I was away for so long in the summer. Grainger did come in about once a week, I think, but he had hardly been at all during the autumn. I did a good deal, myself."

"Pity to let it go," said her father. "If we're going to sell, we ought to have it looking presentable. I'll speak to Grainger. Makes all the difference, the state of the garden, to prospective buyers."

There was much talk of their future plans for settling in Trinidad, and very little was said about Susan's engagement. However, Giles was immediately invited to stay for the coming week-end, and his visit proved an entire success. Mr. Brockley, who was no fool, however selfish he might be, saw at once that Giles was exactly the man to take Susan off his hands. Besides, he had always wanted a son, and here was one ready-made, not only self-supporting, but eminently successful. A man of the world, too, the sort of fellow with whom you could discuss affairs in general.

"Does your father always hold forth at such length?" Giles asked Susan, when they were alone.

She laughed.

"Of course not. You've made quite a hit with him," she answered. "He only gives out his world surveys to people he respects. When it's just Mummy and me he hardly utters."

"Shame."

On Sunday Mrs. Brockley had a "serious" talk with Giles, which he bore patiently. As a result of it the wedding was fixed for the end of January. This news was made general in the evening, and the conversation naturally led on to the prospective guests and the question of relations.

"I suppose we ought to ask Henry," said Susan, "but I'm sure he won't come."

"Of course not," said Mrs. Brockley. "He's in mourning. It's no good asking his mother, either."

"*His mother!*" Giles and Susan exclaimed together.

"Yes. She isn't dead, is she? I never heard she'd died."

"She wasn't there," Susan began, but Giles cut in.

"Did she turn up for Miriam's wedding?" he asked, eagerly.

"No." Mrs. Brockley was indignant. "Poor Henry, we thought it was such a shame. You see, there was only Miriam's father. Her mother had been divorced when she was quite small. And her father made it a very small affair altogether. He was still angry with Miriam, because she'd broken two previous engagements, when he'd made all the arrangements and invited everyone, and so on. I think he expected her to do it again, and was determined not to be let in for such a fiasco a third time."

She looked severely at Susan, who smiled.

"I guarantee not to copy her," she said, glancing at Giles.

"So it was rather a dismal little affair. Only near relations and very close friends. Which made Mrs. Davenport's absence rather too noticeable. Apparently she'd told Henry if he insisted on marrying an Englishwoman she would have nothing to do with her whatsoever. She was quite capable of carrying out that threat. My poor brother made the mistake of his life when he married her."

"That accounts for her not being at the château, then," said Susan. "Poor thing, I wonder if she is living alone somewhere?"

"I expect so. Though it was her own personal property. I'm surprised she made it over to him. They're usually so tenacious, these provincial Frenchwomen."

"No. Wait a bit." Giles was even more excited. "Did you go to your brother's wedding, Mrs. Brockley?"

"No. I didn't. It was too difficult. Just after the First World War. And besides, she was a Catholic and my parents disapproved. I was only in my teens; I had to go by what they ruled."

"The entente seems to have been far from cordial all round," said Susan.

"Did you never see her, then?" Giles insisted.

"No."

"But at least you must know her name. Her Christian name?"

"I did know. Let me see. Basil, can you remember it?"

"Francine," said Mr. Brockley.

Giles drew a long breath.

"So that accounts for it," he said, slowly.

"For what?" Susan asked, in a faint voice.

"For the fact that you didn't have oysters for lunch the day Miriam fell."

CHAPTER XIX

MADAME FRANCINE TURNED the handle of the library door and paused, listening. Then she went in.

"Dinner is ready, my child."

"Don't wait for me. I'm not hungry."

"You are never hungry."

Her eyes went round the room. The fire was bright and warm: she had made it up herself. He sat at his desk, with a table lamp throwing down a circle of light upon the half-filled sheet of paper under his hand. Beyond, the windows were bare, uncurtained, and misted over by the heat within and the frost outside.

She moved across the room to pull the heavy worn velvet into place, then turned to him again, with the same remorseless persistence.

"Dinner is ready."

His pencil dropped from a listless hand.

"You must make an effort, Henri. You eat nothing. You do nothing. Every day it's the same thing."

"I work."

"You work. You say that, but nothing goes out to the publisher. Not even to the Press."

"The work is not finished."

"But you began . . . It is now February. You began— before Christmas."

"I began the day after Miriam's funeral."

She made a gesture of repudiation with both hands, pushing them out from her strong body as if she were trying to hold off some great weight that threatened to crush her.

"I do not want to remember that time," she said, breathing hard.

Henry got up and stood with his back to the fire.

"Why not? It was no grief to you when she died. It was what you had desired for years, and planned, and finally accomplished."

Madame Francine turned away.

"Dinner is ready," she said. "You must come or it will be spoilt."

"No!"

She stopped moving, checked by the fury in his voice, attacking her ponderous obstinacy in the same tones as his father had sometimes used. But she did not turn round.

"Do you know what I am writing? What I have been writing for three months? It is an account of how you murdered my wife."

That brought her round to face him. As he went on speaking, she grew pale, her eyes narrowed, her mouth closed into a thin line of resistance. She was not afraid, and she let him run on, because she must know how much he had found out, and what the danger amounted to.

"You ruled Penguerrec too long. It went to your head. Madame Francine, chief of the maquis. Oh, I know it was necessary to suppress your real name when the Germans arrived. Madame Davenport, the wife of an Englishman, would have been interned at once. So Madame Davenport had left her husband years before, whereabouts unknown, and Madame Francine was housekeeper at the château. The children of Penguerrec forgot they had ever called her by another name. Newcomers never heard any other. Her wartime successes, her wartime murders . . ."

"It was war!" cried Madame Francine, stung into speech at last. "It is not murder to kill an enemy."

"There is a distinction," answered Henry, with a bitter smile, "between a personal enemy and an enemy of the country. There is a difference between suffering for one's own acts against the enemy, and allowing the innocent to suffer."

"You speak like a fool! If I had not preserved my own liberty and life, who would have organised the resistance here in Penguerrec?"

"No one is indispensable. Penguerrec is one small village, not the whole of France."

"We need not quarrel over the part I played. Others thought

more highly of it than you, my own son. But you were corrupted by your father."

"And you by your wicked prejudice. So that in the end, you murdered your own daughter."

"Ah, that, no! Now you prove you are mad, quite mad! Miriam, my daughter! Never! Never!"

Henry pointed an accusing finger at her, his face twisted with pain. "That was the beginning of your crime. Why could you not accept her? She was beautiful, she was my wife, I loved her. If you had made her welcome, if you had become her mother, she would have been different. Her own mother had left her when she was a child. She needed a mother, to help her to grow up. She would have been happy. She would have had children—your grandchildren. We could all have been happy . . ."

"Stop! You are inventing a picture that could never have developed. She was incapable of change. Her character was bad, fundamentally bad. She was a . . ."

Henry moved to strike the foul words from her mouth, but she caught his arm and held him, until his feeble strength ebbed and he sank back again into his chair, his head on his arms.

"You accuse me of the crime of not making her welcome," said Madame Francine, in a terrible voice. "But I warned you I would not receive any Englishwoman here as my daughter-in-law. I warned you that if you brought her I must be housekeeper and nothing else, until you took her away again. But you stayed for eight years. Why? Why did you ever come?"

Henry answered, with bitter shame in his voice, "Because she thought the place was mine. She married me to be a grand lady living in a château. Childish? Of course. She was a child. A beautiful child. I loved her and I could not lose her for want of a little deception, that I hoped to resolve in time."

"You should have known your mother better."

"I should have known you better."

A long silence dragged between them. It was broken by Francine.

"You have no proof."

"I have enough. Some of my friends were approached by Louis. He was always your chief lieutenant, or accomplice. He set the traps. He paid the men who tampered with the yacht."

"It was to drive them away. To frighten them into taking her. You would not take her away, yourself."

"How could I? Without money?"

"There was no need to spend everything you had on her."

"My illness? My doctor's bills?"

"She took the money. You know it. She was insatiable. I did what I did to save you. I wanted to frighten her away before she destroyed you."

"You succeeded. She was mad with fear."

"She tried to murder you."

"Because she blamed me. You allowed that to happen. She might have killed me, because you would not give up your purpose. You were ready to sacrifice your only son to this purpose of saving him. I think it is you that is mad."

Even her obstinacy was shaken a little by this.

"Why did she not go?" she wailed. "Why were those English so indifferent, so stupid, so cold?"

"Why do you repeat these out-worn platitudes, like an old parrot? You know nothing about English people. I cannot imagine why you married my father. Or why he married you."

She was silent, then, but not for long.

"You have no proof! At the end, it was her own doing."

"I have enough. You wore my boots to go down to the stage; to take away the rope; to dig out the foot of the ladder. Oh, yes, Louis says he did it all, as a first step in preparing to mend the ladder. He had no idea that anyone would want to use it that day. He actually showed Renaud all this."

"You see. Nobody would believe your story. You have no proof."

"I know, and Marie and Lucette know, that Louis did not go down through the woods that afternoon. And I did not go; I was with the sergeant of police. But I know, and Giles Armitage knows, that my boots were used. The mud on them was fresh."

"You had come ashore across the mud."

"I was carried ashore," said Henry, "and Inspector Renaud was watching."

Madame Francine stiffened. But she did not give in.

"Has the Englishman, Armitage, spoken?"

"I have not been accused. So I imagine, not."

"In your account, you accuse me?"

"In my account, I describe your crime, and confess my own suspicions of it and my cowardly inaction."

"When will it be finished?"

"Very soon. Unless you kill me first."

A little pitying smile appeared at the corners of her mouth.

"And if I destroy the papers, instead?"

"I will write it again. And again, if necessary. In the end, it will be finished. You will not be safe until I die."

"Are you asking me to kill you, my son?"

"I want to be with Miriam, my wife, my love. You will not be safe or happy until I am dead."

"*Happy!*"

That broke her at last. She found her way to the door and went out, and shut it behind her, leaning against it with her forehead pressed to the wood, in an agony of despair. Her defeat was total, her myth of herself broken and withered. She was alone: she who had never been alone in Penguerrec, but always commanded a faithful following, as far back into childhood as she could remember. She had lost their support by her own actions. They had approved the hunting of Miriam, but the kill had shocked them. They had grown soft. They condemned her. They turned from her. In the village no one would speak to her. That was bad, but at home it was worse. She had fought to possess her son, and she had lost him for ever. Nothing remained. No hope. No future.

After a time the old woman pulled herself away from the door and went into the dining-room, where the soup lay waiting, cold and congealed in the bowl. She sat down in her place at the head of the table, and taking up the carving-knife bared her left wrist. There was nothing left now in her life. It was time to go.

But she paused, the big knife swaying in the air. It was not that she lacked courage: excess of it had brought her to her present predicament. But a thought had come to her, compelling attention from her shrewd, deeply superstitious mind. Miriam had confessed her sins, repented, died in grace. She would have a long purgatory, but in the end, in the far future, she would be joined with Henry in paradise. But for herself, a suicide, damned eternally, there would be no such reunion. She had lost the battle on earth; or rather, had gained an empty victory; she would not be trapped into losing it, finally and forever, in the world to come.

She laid down the carving-knife, and rising from her chair, took up the tureen of soup and carried it away to the kitchen to heat it again for the meal.

In the library, Henry gathered the sheets of his writing together, tore them across, as he had done so many times already, and carrying them to the fire, dropped the pieces into the flames one by one. When the whole surface of the fire was darkened by twisted brittle screws of burned paper, he took the poker and beat them into dust, and threw on another log and waited for new golden flames to spring out of it. Then he went back to his desk, drew out a fresh sheet of paper, and began to write.

THE END